Pig-Out Inn

Pig-Out Inn

Lois Ruby

Houghton Mifflin Company
Boston 1987

Library of Congress Cataloging-in-Publication Data

Ruby, Lois.
  Pig-Out Inn.

  Summary: Spending a summer helping her mother run
a truckstop diner, fourteen-year-old Dovi becomes in-
volved in a custody battle between divorced parents
who both want to hold on to their young son.
  [1. Restaurants, lunchrooms, etc.—Fiction.
2. Divorce—Fiction. 3. Family problems—Fiction]
I. Title.
PZ7.R8314Pi 1987   [Fic]   86-21433
ISBN 0-395-42714-2

Printed in the United States of America

P 10 9 8 7 6 5 4 3 2 1

For Benjamin, Aviva and Kalervo

Pig-Out Inn

ONE

wwwwwwwwwwwwwwwwwwwwwwwwwwwwwwwwwwwwwwwww

Of course, Pig-Out Inn wasn't what it said on the neon
sign out front. Klondike Cafe and Cottages was the
name. Momma looked up the whole case history of this
place before we made our down payment. She went
down to the Spinner Town Hall, where no one had
looked up anything in probably twenty years, and the
town clerk was just thrilled. She gave Momma a pile
of yellowed papers. We found out that the buildings
went up the summer of '54, when it never fell below
100° for twenty-nine consecutive days. So the Klondike
name must have been a joke of the carpenters.

The first time I walked into the diner and saw the
flouncy pink curtains and the overstuffed, lopsided hot
pink booths, I thought it looked like a place where the
Three Little Pigs would have supper. I was hooked. I

picked up a gummy, dog-eared menu, scratched out KLONDIKE, and wrote in its place PIG-OUT INN. I happen to be a world class pig lover. I've got stuffed, glass, wooden, pewter, plastic, and paper pigs of all persuasions. I even have a hand-knitted pig, and a purple one that's big enough for a nursery school kid to ride.

As soon as we moved into the Pig-Out Inn I started decorating the shelves and walls and booths with my personal collection. On every wall there was a poster of a pair of pigs caressing each other's snouts, or pigs rolling in the mud, or pigs holding cloven hoofs and dancing with big pink bows on their curlicues. Johnny, our cook, said it was all disgusting, but there was no question, when the customers started coming in, that this was pig country, and that they were lunching at the Pig-Out Inn.

That's what we called it, from the first day on, in our restaurant family. The family includes my mother, my father (who services computer hardware), and Johnny (who isn't a relative, but is the one professional, since he once took a course in hotel and restaurant management at Butler County Community College). And me.

I am Dovi Chandler, age fourteen. If Dovi seems like an odd name, it's an improvement over what my mother first had in mind: Dove-of-Peace Chandler. My parents are half-baked Quakers (officially called Friends), but even for Quakers, my father said, Dove-of-Peace was carrying things too far. He thought Dovi would be quite enough to make the statement.

The name confused my teachers. My first-grade teacher in Kansas City insisted on pronouncing it Dough-vee. By third grade, in Salina, I was called Duv. I had a teacher in Dallas who insisted on the European pronunciation, Duh-*vee*, which she invented. By the time I hit eighth grade in Wichita I insisted on the original, but it's a stupid name and I'll probably change it if I ever move to New York. *Dominique.* How does that sound?

We move around a lot. We're restless people. My parents met at Friends University in Wichita and were married before they got their bachelor's degrees. I wasn't too alert yet, but I hear we managed an apartment house near the campus, in exchange for free rent. But my mother kept forgetting to collect the rent from the tenants, and my father didn't know much about plumbing (who does?), so he went to work for NCR, National Cash Register, learning computer hardware.

Then my mother heard she could get a Tupperware distributorship in Kansas City, and she'd supervise a whole flock of eager saleswomen. She learned to burp Tupperware to get all the air out of the lettuce crisper and so forth, but she never learned to love Tupperware. Then she got wind of a venture in Salina, a bookstore that was going broke. It came with a cozy building — an old house with a fireplace — and a complete inventory of books. All it needed (the owners said) was fresh capital and some sound management.

Well, we didn't know much about capital, except what we could borrow, or management either, but my mother sure knew books, and we all read a lot, so we loaded everything we owned into the station wagon and drove to Salina. We lived above the bookstore. The only problem was, I don't think anyone in Salina read, or at least read things that didn't come in paperback from the grocery store, and we ended up having to sell the station wagon along with the bookstore.

Dad has a great talent for computer hardware, and he can always find a job. So the next stop was Dallas, where Dad went to work for IBM, and Momma learned to make beeswax candles in a little shop next to Neiman-Marcus, which is a very fancy department store. Momma liked the beeswax, but she couldn't tolerate the customers from Neiman's, and she wasn't sure that beeswax did much for the human condition

4

anyway, so at the end of the school year we went back to Wichita and NCR.

I was thirteen, not quite obese, but far from scrawny. Tacos and fries were my downfall. Momma and I ate out a lot while my father was on the road fixing computers. We were in a mom-and-pop restaurant on Twenty-first Street in Wichita, slicing through a bowl of heavy-duty chili, when my mother said, "You know, Dovi, it wouldn't take much to run a place like this."

I glanced over at Mom and Pop. Pop had a bald head glistening with sweat as he hovered over the steam table; Mom had purple varicose veins, and she shuffled from table to table, filling sugar dispensers.

"A few decent recipes, a consistent method of ordering supplies," my mother said, "a little imagination. Oh, and plenty of change in the cash register. We'll have to remember to get rolls of nickels and dimes and pennies from the bank."

"Are you telling me we're going into the restaurant business?" I asked, not a bit surprised.

"Hmm . . . You remember Johnny, don't you?" Pop came and refilled our iced tea. His apron was splattered with gravy. Mom shuffled to the phone, which Pop didn't even seem to hear.

"Six A.M.," she barked. "Eight P.M. Well, what time

did you *want* to eat?" She slammed the receiver down.

"Johnny Buttons, from the apartment complex. Do you remember him, Dovi? He was the one with the brown Brillo-Pad hair, the one who never paid his utility bills, and then had a fit when they cut off his lights, remember?"

"Sort of."

"He went over to El Dorado for a restaurant course. I think I'll just give Johnny a call." She pushed back her chair, which scraped across the worn wooden floor.

"Can it wait till we get home?" I asked. Pop was slapping the Venetian blinds shut and glaring at the clock every time we looked in his direction.

"Oh, certainly," Momma said. Her head was spinning, and I read the familiar signs clearly.

Goodbye Wichita, goodbye hanging around Towne East Square, goodbye air-conditioned apartment, goodbye two years in a row at the same school, goodbye friends. I knew we'd be in the restaurant business by summer.

Sure enough, as soon as school was out, I slammed shut the yearbook that all my friends had signed (*See you next year, and don't sweat too hard all summer, Love, Dorrie . . . To the smartest girl in school. I like you even though you get A's in algebra, ha ha ha! Love ya, Maria*). I closed my eyes to try to forget their faces. Already I couldn't remember whether Maria had blue or brown eyes. I probably wouldn't ever open the yearbook again. Besides, next year I'd have a Spinner High School yearbook to pile on top of the others.

TWO

〰〰〰〰〰〰〰〰〰〰〰〰〰〰〰〰〰〰〰〰〰〰〰〰

While we were waiting for the Pig-Out Inn to fall into our hands, Momma and Dad discussed details. "We'll order white nylon uniforms," Momma said, but eyeing me with a frown, she changed her mind. "No, white isn't Dovi's color. How about pink, to match the curtains?"

"Listen, guys," I said, "why don't we just wear jeans with whatever we've got on, on top?"

Momma shook her head. "It wouldn't look professional."

"But it would be cheap," Dad reminded her.

"Well . . ." Momma began, weakening slightly. "Maybe jeans and a white shirt. Oh, and a cute red cowboy hankie tied around our necks."

"I'm glad I don't have to dress up that way," my father said, laughing, "like a rodeo dropout."

"Oh, Mike, you're such a stick-in-the-mud." Momma stood on her tiptoes to kiss Dad's neck. "You'll love the restaurant business, I just know it." Momma flirted and pouted, but Dad stood firm for once.

"I'm never giving up NCR again. We need some steady income while you're blowing our money out here, Marilyn."

So we agreed to let Dad stay in a rooming house in Wichita and come out to Spinner every so often on the weekends. He didn't really think we'd be in Spinner too long before we lost our shirts *and* our neckerchiefs.

"I am inordinately fond of uniforms," Momma said dreamily. "But you're right, I guess. Dovi would look better in jeans."

Uniforms are one thing, but clothes in general mean nothing to Momma, maybe because she's the sort of lady who looks terrific in anything. I've seen pictures of her when miniskirts were in, and she looked like a darling little plaything. Then, when long skirts were the fashion, she'd make a point of spinning around and having the bottom of the skirt swish around her, like it was late in catching up. She could also look sophisticated and businesslike when she had to in a gray flannel suit, like the day she went for the reading of my grandfather's will. Incidentally, he left her a few thousand dollars, which is what we used for the down payment on the Pig-Out.

Jeans? Oh, Momma's a knockout in jeans, with her tight little hind end and long cowgirl legs. She isn't that tall, but she's all legs. People look at her, then at me, and figure I'm adopted.

My hair is lighter than Momma's by three shades on the Miss Clairol chart, and you'd think my pants were leaded the way everything seems to sink to the bottom. Elsewhere, the news is better. I look pretty good in a sweater — meaty, but not jiggly. Where other girls pride themselves on a flat belly or silky hair or a dainty pair of ankles, I've always thought that my most gorgeous feature is my hands. I've got naturally perfect nails, which comes from lots of homogenized milk and Jell-O, and I've got these long fingers that I tend to curl in toward my thumb to emphasize a point.

My hands are so extraordinary that my sixth-grade teacher picked me to sign the whole Christmas pageant, even though I didn't know a word of sign at that point and two other sixth graders did, including a deaf one. In fact, while I'm laying it on so thick, I'll just mention that my mother heard about this modeling agency up in Omaha that's looking for hands for jewelry commercials, and she sent them pictures of my disembodied hands. But no word's come back yet.

As for the rest of me — well, I have the usual number of eyes and lips and so forth on my face, arranged in the customary pattern. I'm not pretty, except to my grandmothers, and I'm not a fright either, though my green eyes fire up when I'm furious, and I take on what my father calls my dragon demeanor.

I am much too fiery to be even a half-baked Quaker, but we're all hoping that maturity will help. Hoping, but not holding our breath.

Johnny is not a Quaker. He's what my father calls a lapsed Methodist, which means he hasn't been to church in twenty-five years, but if he had gone in all that time, it would have been to a Methodist church, probably. Johnny is a blustery tyrant but, underneath it all, a pretty good man. Johnny is *not* a good cook, however.

That was our first surprise when we opened the Pig-Out. Sure, Johnny studied about how to select cantaloupes at Butler County Community College, and how to design cute menus, and how to apply for a liquor license, but he never quite learned to cook.

"What the hey are you supposed to do with these

slickies?" he asked, squishing five pounds of stewed tomatoes around in his hands.

"With a little of this, and a little of that," Momma explained patiently, "they will magically turn into spaghetti sauce."

Momma wasn't much of a cook either. But we had the famous Betty Crocker cookbook, and our first lesson was from the section "Cooking for Crowds." I read aloud, Momma chopped and measured things, and Johnny performed the final artistic steps, such as moving the ten-gallon pots from the counter to the stove. Our first creation was a nine-pound gristly mess of chili that we put in the refrigerator and scraped three inches of grease off of the next morning. Then Betty Crocker told us how to bleed off the grease while it was still hot so that, voilà! we could serve Johnny's chili same-day fresh.

Truckers like chili; chili, chicken-fried steak, pork tenderloin, and hamburgers. Johnny, of course, hadn't ever cooked any of these, but Momma said, "Truck drivers are the salt of the earth. Let's feed them what they like best, because the whole country depends on them to get goods from one point to another, and nobody, *nobody* can drive with indigestion."

We quickly got to know the regular customers,

who'd seen probably six owners of the Klondike and were now training the world's first Pig-Out Inn owners.

There was Palmer, from the gas station across the street, whose wife was known as the worst cook in Wellington County. The other interesting thing about Palmer was that he had absolutely no sense of humor. None. Then there was Emile Joe Hunter, a trucker for P.I.E. who couldn't digest raw vegetables because of some operation he'd had once to lose weight, but it obviously hadn't done any good.

Emile Joe would get insulted when Johnny accidentally put lettuce on his sandwich, as if we were trying to poison him. "I'm never stopping here again," he'd bark, and his jowls would shake just like a bulldog's. "Cook ought to be able to remember a simple thing like hold the lettuce." But Emile Joe would come back time after time, because truck drivers have a real feeling for tradition, and the Pig-Out was like home to them.

Another regular was Pap Morgan, and every couple of days a man named Pawnee — maybe he was an Indian — stopped in and dumped a few complaints on us. Barbara and Bill Wanamaker, who shared the driving, would drop in for a cold drink or hot coffee now and then, and they'd bring in their sweaty baby in one of those pink plastic carriers that looked like a serving tray. They didn't eat much at our place because they were out to make a quick killing on the road before the baby got too big.

Here's how a typical on-the-job training session would go:

"The coffee's got to be thick as mud. You got to be able to taste the caffeine," Bill Wanamaker told us. Like most truckers, Bill's left arm was a lot darker than his right. His right arm had a tic-tac-toe board tattooed on it, maybe that's how he and Barbara passed the hours on the road. "If you don't keep the coffee strong we're gonna be asleep at the wheel, and it's gonna make a bloody mess on the highway."

"Hey, all you and your wife are hauling is peaches," Pawnee said. "How 'bout if I splattered my load over the highway — dead sheep lying all over the place? The highway patrol would have to send out a crane to get those babies up off the highway before they started to smell."

"Aw, come on, Pawnee," Barbara Wanamaker moaned from a back booth. She was nursing the baby and had her back to us. She had pretty sun-bleached hair to her shoulders and jeans so tight that I wondered how she could bend her legs. "You're not going to kill a whole load of three-hundred-pound sheep with one crash."

"Could," Pawnee said defensively. "It's up to Dovi here. You keep that coffee fresh and hot and thick."

"And tell that cook you've got back there," Emile Joe said, "that it turns my stomach when he fries the hot cakes after the bacon. It repeats on me all the way to St. Louis, so I'm always chewing Tums. Oh, and be sure to stock plenty of Tums, unless the cook's gonna improve a whole lot in the next few weeks."

"What's he talking about with the bacon grease?" Pap Morgan said. "I'll tell you what's missing from your menu." He pulled one out from behind the ketchup bottle, flipped it open, and pointed to a blank spot. I tried to read what wasn't there, upside down. "Biscuits and red-eye gravy, that's what's missing."

I didn't like the sound of it, but there was this sign on the wall that proclaimed "The Two Rules of Business," and it said,

1. The customer is always right.
2. If the customer is wrong, refer to Rule 1.

So I asked about red-eye gravy.

"Simple," Pap Morgan explained. "You fry up the bacon in a big black skillet. You never, ever wash out a cast iron skillet. Just scrape it out with paper towels.

So, you fry up the bacon, then you pour a little flour into the grease after the bacon's out, and you mix it up good to thicken it, and while it's piping hot you pour it over fresh biscuits. It's out of this world. Hangs in the gut for the whole trip, too."

"Why's it called red-eye?" I asked.

"Plain and simple, it's the bacon flecks that look like your standard bloodshot eye. Best stuff I ever put my tongue to."

We penciled it in on the menus, and it was a hit. I tasted just the tip of a spoonful of it once and gagged.

THREE

The first few weeks in the restaurant business were tough but not hard, as I used to say about the times tables in fourth grade. I think fourth grade was in Chillicothe, Missouri, but I may be wrong on that.

Well, the point is, we had good teachers and learned pretty fast how to run a place like the Pig-Out, which is why we weren't blown right out of the water on our second Saturday, when the Army landed.

At eleven o'clock that morning a convoy of three trucks pulled up into our parking lot and dumped out thirty-two khaki-clad men. All of them were hungry and wanted hamburgers and shakes. All of them also wanted the key to the men's room.

"Forty-eight burgers, Johnny," I yelled into the pass-through window. "Six well, fourteen medium, twenty-three medium rare, and five still breathing."

I heard Johnny muttering to himself back there. "Slap the burgers on the grill, Johnny." Plop, plop, plop; a row of flat little pellets dropped onto the sizzling grill. "Grease the buns, Johnny," he reminded himself. "Buns. Holy shee, Marilyn, who expected the whole U.S. Army?"

"Hold your horses, Johnny," Momma said calmly, poking her head into the pass-through. "I'll send Dovi to the walk-in for more buns."

Ordinarily I did not like the walk-in freezer. It made my head ache right behind my ears if I stayed in there too long, which I had a tendency to do when things got hectic out front. But that day I didn't mind the walk-in because it was at least 99° in the restaurant kitchen, and 109° outside. You had to walk out the back door and across this gravelly place to get to the freezer. If you didn't have shoes on, you ran, or else you fried the bottoms of your feet. My mother said I ought to be able to take slightly crisp feet. She saw a yogi once, a guy who wore a diaper, like, and who danced across some hot coals, but they couldn't have been as hot as rocks baking in the Kansas summer sun.

Well, anybody with half a brain wouldn't go barefoot from the kitchen to the walk-in, and besides, there was a law against working in the diner in bare feet. They must have thought your feet had more germs than your nose or something, which is ridiculous, because anyone who's taken your basic eighth-grade life science, like I did last year, knows about the diseases you get from the dripping human nose.

But, as my father says, I digress.

So, I pulled six dozen buns from the freezer and pushed the walk-in door shut with my hind end, the same one I used to keep the screen door from banging in the kitchen. "Here you go, Johnny. You're back in business." I could hardly see him over the smoke from the burgers.

"What am I gonna do with iceberg buns? My burgers are ready to walk," Johnny roared. He roared because the Army was so loud in the other room, and he roared because he usually roared.

"Relax," my mother crooned, with four feet of foil betweeen her and the dispenser. "We'll wrap them up and put them in the oven." She turned the oven up to 500°. "They'll be warm in no time." Warm? It was hot enough without the oven to fry burgers right on the counter.

Well, next we had to face the milkshake ordeal, so Momma and I started an assembly line: squirt the syrup into the bottom of the four metal cups, plop the ice cream in, pour on the milk, shove the whole mess up into the mixer, and who cared what splattered all over the counter and wall because there were always four more milkshakes to go.

The Army guys could have helped, but oh no. They sat around with their knees spread like sailors and their feet wrapped around the bottoms of the stools, or else they shoved each other around in the booths, or pounded the juke box to coax out at least twelve quarters' worth of country, everything from Tammy to Willie singing about being on the road again, which is where we wished the Army was.

And the toilet kept flushing. "We'll go broke on the water alone," my mother moaned into the strawberry syrup.

I passed out milkshakes like I was dealing poker.

"Hey, this isn't chocolate," one guy complained. He couldn't have been much older than I was.

"Hu-uh. We're doing all the strawberries now."

"But I ordered chocolate."

"Well then, trade with somebody," I said impatiently.

"But you haven't done any chocolates yet," the next guy reminded me.

"Please, mister, please, don't play B-17," Olivia pleaded from the juke box. I grabbed the shake away from the kid. "Who ordered a strawberry?" By now my mother had four more shakes ready. Oh, we were

20

rolling. But we were way behind in sloshing mayonnaise on the buns, and then there were the onions and pickles to think about as Johnny piled up naked burger plates on the pass-through.

Momma dashed over to drop a few chips on each plate, and we started sliding them down the counter to the first soldier on the end.

"This is a real class joint," said some guy smashed in the back of a booth.

"Anything for our men in uniform," Momma said sweetly. She was the one who used to counsel draft resisters during Vietnam. Those days, everyone she touched ended up in Canada or in jail. A new flock of burgers came tumbling out with top buns toasted crisp and bottoms soggy wet, but who had time to worry?

We were on the vanilla shakes now, and both Momma and I were sticky to the elbows.

"You picked a sad time to leave me, Lucille," wailed Kenny from the juke box.

"Lucille had a lot of common sense," Momma muttered.

In spite of Johnny's hamburgers, the Army wanted dessert. They cleaned us out of banana cream pie and chocolate layer cake and were settling for our famous

Baby Ruths, which had been around so long that if you tried to snap one in two it would bend like a boomerang.

Everyone said that the food and service were terrible, and that they'd be back the next Saturday, and finally the invasion was over, less than an hour after it started. Momma and I were left to sort through the rubble. There were ketchup and mustard puddles everywhere, pickles plastered to the tables, peanuts from Baby Ruths ground into the floor, and potato chip crumbs working their way down into the cracks between the backs and seats of the booths.

Momma wiped her hands on her apron, which did no good because little rivers of ice cream were dried all the way down her arm. "We could apply for a grant as a disaster area," she said, while Johnny slammed dishes around in the big washtubs in the kitchen. "You know, Dovi, sometimes I think we're not suited to being restaurateurs."

"Holy shee," Johnny yelled. "Getta loada this." We both dashed into the kitchen, and there was Johnny holding up a plate at arm's distance. On the plate was a plastic and wire pink thing that looked like false teeth, only it had no teeth. I recognized it, because I saw half a dozen just like it every day in the lunchroom at my last school. Dorrie even wore one.

"That's a retainer," I said, laughing.

"What the hey does it retain?" asked Johnny, disgusted.

"Teeth. After the orthodontist is through with them." I was guessing that it belonged to that one kid who didn't order strawberry. "I'll just wrap it up in a napkin. He'll be back for it."

"Naw, he won't," Johnny said. "Uncle Sam'll buy him another one."

Momma was genuinely puzzled. "Why would a boy who isn't even through getting his teeth straightened be in the Army?"

Johnny brushed her off. He never understood her depth. "Aw, the kid's joined up to see the world."

"This is the world, all right. Spinner, Kansas," I hissed, "home of the world famous Pig-Out Inn."

Any driver who was going to eat at the world famous Pig-Out Inn had usually already done so by eight o'clock at night, so we'd clean up and collapse in the back booth with a hot fudge banana split that would have fed half the orphans in Laos. That night, after the Army invasion, Momma and I were racing each other through the ice cream when our first certifiable weirdo came in.

It was nine o'clock, just at closing time. I'd already

dumped the coffee grounds out of the huge pot and was wrestling it into the sink. Naturally, I protected my hands with rubber gloves. Johnny was clattering pots and pans in the kitchen, and Momma had all the day's money spread out in the back booth. So in walks this guy we'd never seen before, and there was something about him that set Momma and me both on edge. He wasn't a trucker; you could tell that by what he was wearing. The best way to describe him is to say he could have starred in one of those nerd movies. He had on a limp, short-sleeved yellow-and-green-and-blue-striped shirt, buttoned at the neck, and brown Goodwill-type pants. He wore his belt two or three notches too tight. Maybe that's why his eyes bulged half out of their sockets. He should have had horn-rimmed glasses, but didn't. What he did have was this fiendish grin, as though his face had been sliced open, or like clay with a slit for a mouth.

One glance at him, and Momma scooped all the money into her apron and slipped into the kitchen. She was back in a flash, with a broom in both her hands. "What'll it be, sir?" she said, holding the broom like a gladiator's shield.

"I'm . . . so . . . thirsty," he said.

"Well, we have Coke, we have Sprite," Momma began prattling nervously. "Iced tea, sugar-free or sweetened, iced coffee. We've got lemonade, we've got orangeade, root beer, Dr. Pepper. Also beer. But we're closing."

"Just a little . . . something to . . . wet the whistle," the man said, and Momma plunked an iced tea down in front of him. "How much?" he asked, reaching into his pocket.

"On the house," said Momma instantly. "It's the bottom of the pot anyway." He smiled even wider, if possible, and started in on his tea in delicate tea party sips, while his fish eyes inspected every corner of the Pig-Out. "I like your . . . little piggies on . . . the wall," he said.

"Dovi, go help Johnny clean up," Momma said firmly. I caught on right away.

In the kitchen, I pulled Johnny away from the pass-through and whispered, "There's somebody really weird out there. Momma thinks he's going to hold us up."

Johnny bent toward the pass-through to give the guy a good look. There was that same diabolical grin plastered on his fishy face.

"Aw, he's harmless," Johnny said. "I've seen my share of weirdos, most of 'em over in Korea, and take it from me, this one's a puppy dog. No problem."

"Just the same, come out in front, will you?"

"I'm cleaning up the kitchen. I'll be here till the sun comes up if I don't get to it."

"Well, I'm not leaving Momma alone out there, even if you are a big coward."

"Women — hysterical broads," Johnny muttered.

Well, after about half an hour the man worked his way down to the bottom of the glass, which wasn't easy to do, smiling the whole time, and then he spooned out a few clinging grains of sugar. Finally, with Momma and me both watching him like a hawk, he said, "Bye-bye, folks. I'll . . . stop by . . . next time I'm . . . passing this way."

Momma and I let out a big sigh of relief when he left, tearing off down the highway on a motor scooter with a funny little sidecar attached to it.

"He's gone, Johnny," we called into the kitchen. "You can come out of hiding."

Johnny went right on scrubbing the grill with a greasy cloth tied over a brick. But he managed to mutter loud enough for us to hear him over the scrape-scraping. "Big deal. A Mafia guy, I can see it. A hood on a Kawasaki, sure. But some poor grinning *de*-fective comes in and they crack into a hundred pieces. Women."

I was furious with Johnny. What ever happened to the pioneer men, protecting their women on the prairie? That's always happening in movies, but in real life? Forget it. I stomped through the swinging doors, glowering at Johnny as I packed up *his* leftover lettuce and *his* leftover tomatoes and had to squeeze them into the jungle of *his* refrigerator. "Hey, what's this?" I pulled out a cool, brown leather thing that sure looked a lot like a wallet.

"Gimme that!" Johnny grabbed it out of my hand and worked it into his back pocket.

"What's your wallet doing in the refrigerator?"

Johnny stammered and snorted.

"Johnny!"

"You think I was going to let that weirdo rip off my wallet? I may be stupid, but I ain't no fool!"

FOUR

∿∿∿∿∿∿∿∿∿∿∿∿∿∿∿∿∿∿∿∿∿∿∿∿∿∿∿∿∿∿∿∿∿∿∿

There was a guy we called C.W. (pronounced "Cee Dubyah") who drove this classy Peterbilt big rig and hauled anhydrous ammonia from St. Louis to Denver. He was huge, and he wore denim overalls like Paul Bunyan, or that guy Big John on the chili can. Cee Dubyah would come into the Pig-Out Inn for lunch a couple of times a week, or if he'd had a late start out of St. Louis he'd stop in for two pieces of coconut cream pie and a box of No-Doz to get him through the night. Every so often he'd take one of the cottages for the night and be gone before sunrise.

Then one day, here comes Cee Dubyah with a kid following behind, both of them walking just the same swaggery way as if they'd just climbed down from prize Arabian stallions.

"This here's Tag," Cee Dubyah announced.

"Hi, Tag," I said, looking the kid over carefully. He was a small, nine-ish version of Cee Dubyah in high-water blue jeans that had the back pockets torn clear off and a U-necked undershirt. He was pretty muscular for a small kid. Maybe he helped Cee Dubyah load trucks, or worked out at the Y. He had freckles all over his face and arms and shoulders, and a rag pile of matted brown hair. Well, it had to be sweaty bouncing down the highway in the Peterbilt — hard on a guy's hair. And he wore a small cross on a chain around his neck.

"Whaddya want, Tag?" Cee Dubyah asked.

"Nuthin." Tag had a deep, raspy voice, like maybe his throat was dry from the truck. He hopped up on a counter stool and crossed one ankle over his other knee, just the way Cee Dubyah did.

"Six hours on the road, and you're not even getting a bite?" Cee Dubyah said. "You must have a lot of fat to live off of." The kid was skinny as a noodle. Cee Dubyah studied the menu, though he must have known it by heart. It never changed from week to week, and neither did he.

"What are you eating?" Tag asked.

"Spaghetti. It's the only thing fit to eat here."

"That's what I'm having," Tag said. "Spaghetti."

"Well, don't be so quick. They've got decent hamburgers," Cee Dubyah said, his face buried in the menu.

"Then that's what I'll have. Spaghetti and a hamburger. Hey, Cee Dubyah, have we got enough money?"

"Oh sure, kid. In fact, we're gonna take us a room tonight right here at the Klondike."

Tag looked around. I got the feeling he wasn't too impressed. But the VACANCY sign outside was flashing yellow streaks on our wall, and the hamburger was sizzling away on the grill, and Tag was sucking foam off the top of his root beer, and I guess he decided it would be okay to stay. "Clean sheets?" he asked.

"Does this look like the kind of place where they'd give you somebody else's sheets?" Cee Dubyah replied.

"We having breakfast too?"

"Right here on that stool you're sitting on. Dovi's putting a reserved sign on it, right, girl?"

"Then tomorrow we hit the road again?" Tag asked with a weak smile. He had these tiny white shark's teeth that looked like they'd snap off in a corn-on-the-cob.

"Well, we'll talk about that in the morning," Cee

Dubyah said. It sure sounded as if he wanted to avoid the subject, so I helped him along by sliding a couple of steaming plates of spaghetti down the counter to the two of them.

I never saw a kid eat so fast. I swear, he looked like a horse eating hay, with that spaghetti hanging out of his mouth. He had a circle of orange around his lips which he tried to wipe off with the back of his hand, but it didn't do any good. Then he snarfed down the hamburger, saving the last two bites to sop up what was left of the spaghetti sauce. Cee Dubyah ordered him a wedge of pie, but two bites into it I could tell he had no use for coconut cream. Cee Dubyah ate from Tag's plate, one delicate bite at a time — as though he were just taking a little bitty taste — while Tag solemnly worked his way through a hot fudge sundae. Watching this kid pack away all that food reminded me of a Saturday morning cartoon I once saw where this giraffe was swallowing his breakfast, and you could see every ball of food jumping down inside his neck. There was Tag, skinny as a noodle, as I said, but his gut was starting to plump up and hang over his belt like a junior-sized beer belly.

Cee Dubyah and Tag didn't talk much while they ate, but there seemed to be an easy silence between them. When one wanted the salt, a wave of the hand was all it took to tell the other to pass it. They were like two men who'd been traveling together forever.

I'm a nosy person, there's no question about it. I'm always getting into trouble sticking my nose in other people's business, and I ask too many questions, and I never have the sense to know when the questions are too personal. So I was dying to know what the story was on Cee Dubyah and Tag.

"Is this your son, Cee Dubyah?" I asked. Good lead-in, right? A question like that could go anywhere.

"Thought I introduced you. Dovi Whatsername, meet my boy Taggert Layton."

Tag stuck his sundae spoon into the ice cream like a flag and offered his hand across the counter. His fingernails were bitten down to the quick and had little ridges of dirt on the chewed-off edges. Definitely not model hands. "Pleased to meetcha," he said. That little kid had a powerhouse shake that left me feeling like a flopping fish.

"Listen, get your ma out here. Me and Tag are gonna need a room for the night."

"Momma! A live one wants to rent a cottage," I shouted into the kitchen. Out came my mother, wiping dishwater off her hands down the side of her jeans.

"Hi, Cee Dubyah. You want your usual one?"

"Is it open for tonight?"

"Is it open?" We all had a good laugh. Every single one of the nine cabins was open. Three of them hadn't been rented at all since last fall, not once. Momma went back into the kitchen and returned with a key on a wooden block: Red Cottage 4, it said. Of course, all the cottages were gray stone. What do you expect — that we looked like Disneyland or something? But they were called Red, Blue, Yellow, and so forth because each cottage had a little set of shutters, and the shutters were painted all those rainbow colors. At night you couldn't tell what color they were, though, so the cottages each had a number, too.

Cee Dubyah paid in advance, as usual, then paid for their dinner, leaving a hefty tip.

"Hey, Cee Dubyah, this is a mistake," I said, staring at the five-dollar tip he left me for a crummy $5.67 dinner bill.

"Naw, keep it." He seemed a little embarrassed. "You've been real helpful to me all the times I come in here," he said. Geez, I'd have to give him royal diplomat service forever, with a tip like that!

Cee Dubyah patted his belly contentedly, and Tag did the same; then Cee Dubyah went over to the cash register for a toothpick, and again Tag did the same; then Cee Dubyah ordered a six-pack of beer to take with him, and that put Tag out of his league, but Cee Dubyah bought him a six-pack of Life Savers (mixed fruit, the worst kind) and they took off for Red Cottage 4.

As usual, Cee Dubyah's truck was gone before the sun came up, so at about nine I went to his cottage to clean up, just in case we happened to get a whole load of people from a bus that broke down or something. And guess what. There was Tag sleeping on his stomach, in his gray underwear; the sheet was kicked to the floor. His jeans were heaped like the dress of the melted Wicked Witch of the West, as though he'd slid out of them and down under the floorboards. A belt buckle stuck up at a funny angle: FFA, FUTURE FARMERS OF AMERICA, it said. I was so surprised to see Tag there that I just kept staring, with clean sheets slung over my arm and a dust mop standing next to me like a dance partner. Pretty soon he opened one eye. Now, any other kid would have jumped up and run for cover, but not Tag.

"What are you here for?" he asked.

"I'm cleaning the place. How about you?"

"Sleeping, can't you tell?"

"Well, Cee Dubyah's gone, so I just wondered."

Tag sat up and glanced around the room. He had this funny way of moving his eyes while he kept his head perfectly still, almost like that portrait of George Washington that has the eyes that follow you wherever you go.

"I knew it. He went and left me here."

"For how long?" I asked.

"I dunno. He won't be gone too long."

"Is Cee Dubyah really your father?" I asked. What kind of a father would leave his kid in a grungy red-shuttered cottage alone?

"Of course he's my father, stupid. Let's see, I gotta have a plan." Tag ran his fingers through his hair, but it took some doing because it was so gnarly.

"You could take a shower and wash your head," I suggested.

Tag's eyes narrowed as he asked, "And what good's that gonna do me?"

"It may not do you much good, but it would sure help the rest of us who have to smell you."

He nodded soberly, and I could see something, some plan of action, forming behind his eyes. He hopped off the bed and started rummaging through the papers on the desk and in the drawers until he found what he was looking for.

"What's that, Tag?"

"A note. I knew Cee Dubyah'd leave me a note." And he pulled a crisp ten-dollar bill out of the envelope. The little brat just sat there reading the note and didn't tell me a word of it. I decided I'd have to sneak back in when Tag was out of the room and see what Cee Dubyah had had to say.

I forgot about Tag for a while because I had to get busy over in Yellow Cottage 6, where I was setting up housekeeping for my cousin Stephanie and me. That afternoon Stephanie was coming in from Wichita to spend a couple of weeks. If she liked the restaurant business, why, she'd just stay all summer. She wasn't my favorite relative in the world, but we all liked her and felt sorry for her because Stephanie's mother was so ordinary, and I thought it wouldn't be too bad having someone near my age to hang around with at the Pig-Out.

Johnny drove me to the bus depot during the afternoon lull. "What the hey," Johnny said. "I got nothing else to do but sit here counting cans of beans and wishing I was fishing in the mountains."

Stephanie was the first one off the bus. She dropped her huge canvas suitcase on Johnny's toe and threw her arms around me. "Dovi Chandler, I thought I'd never see you again. I mean, I've missed you *sooo* much. I brought a yearbook to show you. I'm in it twelve times!"

"I know, I know; I was there when you counted. Remember?"

She gave me a painfully patient glare. "Yes, Dovi, but that was before *Him*. After *Him*, everything changed."

"Him Larry, or Him Scott?"

Stephanie shoved me away for a second. "We — are — out — of touch. "Didn't I write you? *Him* is Wayne Firestone. You didn't know him because, of course, you were only an eighth grader. Wayne was a freshman."

"This is Johnny," I said. "He's a senior." Johnny grunted and picked up Stephanie's suitcase. Well, old Johnny was hardly competition for someone as wonderful as *The* Wayne Firestone, but Stephanie let him take her suitcase anyway, acting as though she'd been brought up with a whole staff of servants. She hadn't; her father was a mailman, and her mother worked the airplane-part assembly line at Boeing.

"Wayne Firestone is already playing baseball for the high school team," Stephanie said, "and he doesn't even start school there until fall. Can you believe it? And he's playing in a summer league. He's a first baseman. A classic left-handed first baseman."

I wondered if we'd get around to talking about anything other than Wayne Firestone. I wanted to tell her about the train depot in Spinner where this old retired railroad man kept his pride and joy, an actual working steam engine and a coach car. He'd stand there in his conductor's uniform all year round, even in the snow, handing out free tickets for kids to climb up into the train and crawl around the engine and blow the whistle and everything. It was even in *Life* magazine. I figured Stephanie would love to hear about the train depot. When I was eleven and she was twelve we saw *Doctor Zhivago* on cable TV four times in one week, and that got us dream-talking about taking a train trip the whole width and breadth of Russia, back at the time of the czars. We'd be the rich people, of course, not the peasants.

But I couldn't get a word in edgewise; Wayne Firestone was apparently the topic of the day. *Du jour*, as my mother said. That and *au jus* were on our menu, but I'm sure people like Cee Dubyah didn't pay any attention to stuff like that.

"He's five foot nine, and he hasn't even had his major growth spurt yet," Stephanie said dreamily. She worried about height, being five seven herself.

"Wayne Firestone," I repeated, nodding as though I could picture him in my mind. But he had a conductor's cap on and warts all across his nose. I wasn't prepared for this new, updated Stephanie, woman of the world. But I should have been; a few weeks can make a big difference at our age. After all, Stephanie was through-and-through a city girl, and in the city they had a Ninth-Grade Graduation and a Ninth-Grade Formal Dinner Dance. Here in Spinner, ninth graders like I was going to be were just the babies in the high school. Baby Cows, they were called; the school mascot was a longhorn steer. Believe it or not, I was looking forward to being a Baby Cow in the fall.

"But you haven't told me anything about what life is like here," Stephanie said, surveying the dingy bus station. Johnny was already out of sight, and I hurried Stephanie along to his pickup.

"You haven't given me a chance," I muttered.

Stephanie hugged me again, slamming her purse against my back. "We just did *You're a Good Man, Charlie Brown* at the Art Association. You would have loved it. I was in charge of props. Oh, and remember Donna Sperling? She broke her leg water-skiing the weekend before we opened. She had to do Lucy in a cast, and it was disgusting what people wrote on it. Oh, I'm so happy to see you, Dov. Wichita just isn't the same without you. Of course, we couldn't be in the same school since I'm going to high school next year and you'll still be in junior high."

"Not here in Spinner. Here we have four-year high schools, the way you're supposed to."

"So this is Spinner, Kansas," Stephanie said, turning this way and that to take it all in. "It's positively a picture postcard!"

She probably thought it was the hick spot of the universe, Hayseed, U.S.A., but to me it looked like a reasonable place to sink some roots. Sometimes, in Kansas City and Chillicothe and Salina and Dallas, I felt a little like a weed. You know how a weed springs up overnight, then grows stronger than the daffodils and tomatoes and starts to take over, until someone yanks it out by the frail roots. Every so often, when I couldn't sleep and lay awake at three o'clock in the morning, I'd have this urge to be a potato, with the best part of me sunk deep into the soil. By dawn I'd come to my senses, though. One look at Stephanie, who'd never lived anywhere but Wichita and who couldn't think of a thing these days besides her love life, was enough to remind me how beautiful and full of surprises some weeds could be.

FIVE

Packed like sardines in Johnny's pickup, it was pretty hard to do much but point out the local sights. "See, we have a McDonald's," I said, "and a Taco Bravo, and a TG&Y five-and-dime just like you do in Wichita."

"Stay away from that taco place," Johnny warned her. "It'll give you food poisoning."

"Oh, come on, Johnny. He's always trying to drum up business for our place. You'll see it, just around the next bend," I said, surprised at this little bubble of pride I felt. "There it is." Right away I saw the Pig-Out through Stephanie's eyes: a little pink shack sort of leaning into the Kansas prairie wind, with a bunch of small square windows across its face and a yellow neon sign stuck at the top of a big clumsy pole. We were always forgetting to turn off the sign in the morning, and now it was flashing KLONDIKE CAFE AND COTTAGES.

"Klondike? You said Pig-Out."

"The girl has pigs on the brain all the time. Yells 'Stop!' every time we pass hogs in a field around here," Johnny grumbled. "To me, pigs are just ham waiting to be sliced up thick."

Stephanie got a sickly look on her face, as though she'd never sat down to a plate of ribs in her life — which she had, with me as a witness, and she got as greasy as the next guy. Or maybe it was the Klondike Cafe that made her look sick.

"This — place — is — a kick!" she cried. "I love it! And I'm so excited about being in the restaurant business with you. Is your mother going to stay here long? Is she going to pay me?"

"Yeah, I'm the only one works for free," Johnny said.

"He does not. She'll pay you, but only minimum wage and only during the peak hours, like eleven to one thirty and five to seven."

Johnny never believed in gradual slowdowns. He pulled into the gravel parking lot and jammed on the brakes. We almost flew through the windshield. "You trying to kill us, Johnny?"

"The thought crossed my mind," he said charitably. "What the hey is that kid doing over there?"

I spotted Tag, wearing a faded green alligator shirt with the back tuck-in end hanging over his rump, wheeling and dealing from a turned-over wooden carton.

"Ice cold beer," he crooned, "ice cold beer right here."

"Who's *that?*" Stephanie asked.

"An orphan. This kid who's been dumped on our doorstep," I said. "His name is Tag." I ran over to him and demanded, "What are you doing?"

"Community service for truck drivers. Picture this," he said in his growly voice, spreading a scene out before us in the sky. "You're coming in off the road, ready to call it a day. Your neck's aching, your back's stiff, your fingers are sore from curling around that wheel, your throat's as dry as Death Valley. An ice cold beer would feel so good sliding down your dusty throat."

"But we sell beer inside," I shouted. "You can't sell it out here and compete with us."

Tag shrugged his shoulders. "It's a free country."

"Besides, you can't sell beer at all. It's against the law at your age."

Tag sighed, pretending to summon up all the patience a saint would need to deal with us. "You see this beer, which I don't mind telling you I only have two left of, out of six? This is the beer you sold Cee Dubyah last night. How old are you?"

"That's none of your business."

"Well, that tells me you're against the law too. You gonna turn me in, or am I gonna turn you in first?" A big ITT diesel semi pulled in just then, and Tag shooed us away. "Ice cold beer, cheap," he sang into the exhaust of the truck. "Taste mighty good going down after a long day on the road, hey mister? No? Well then, how 'bout some Life Savers?"

"This is too much," said Stephanie. "Nothing like this ever happens in Wichita!"

It was nearly four thirty. We had just enough time to get Stephanie's things into Yellow Cottage 6, grab aprons, and face the dinner crowd; I'd have to deal with Tag later. Stephanie changed into some jeans and a T-shirt, and I took her into the cafe for her first taste of the restaurant business. Momma came running out of the kitchen and threw her arms around Stephanie. "You've grown so much, sweetie."

"I hope I stop soon. I'm taller than half the boys at school," Stephanie said sadly.

"Oh, this good country air will slow down your growth," Momma said.

"Why?" Stephanie asked, puzzled.

"It seems logical," said Momma. My mother was intelligent, but certainly not at all logical. Still, she always believed everything she said. "You'll see. You'll be at least two inches shorter when you leave Spinner, but I can only guarantee it if you stay all summer."

"Aunt Marilyn, you haven't changed a bit," Stephanie beamed. "My mother is so terminally middle-aged. How could you possibly be sisters?"

"Your mother does PTA. That explains it," Momma said.

I showed Stephanie the station where we kept the silverware and the napkins and salt and peppers and sugars, and I gave her a crash course in using our ancient cash register, and I showed her the menu and told her what we were out of, like baked fish, which we hadn't had since we opened because Johnny didn't like the smell of fish. We were both squatting down, checking out the contents of the little fridge under the counter, when the bell above the door tinkled.

"Omigosh, my first customer," Stephanie whispered. "Do you think I'm ready?"

"Oh sure," I whispered back. "You've seen it done in movies a thousand times." Then she stood up, twisted around a little bit to get her T-shirt just right, and flashed this incredible charm.

"Good evening. What'll it be?"

The guy was Palmer, from the gas station across the street. He always had a little something here before he went home to dinner. He was the one whose wife was the worst cook in the county, and a mean old bird besides.

Palmer said, "What's with that kid out there? He come into my place this afternoon begging for some ice. I told him, 'I don't give ice away.' He wants to pay $1.29, I'll give him a sack. But no, he said he had no use for a whole sack. Just needed enough to keep a few cans cold. I said I wasn't opening up a ten-pound sack of ice to give him a handful. So the kid said, 'Okay, let's make a deal.'"

"Uh, sir, would you care to order from our dinner menu?" Stephanie said, batting her eyelashes.

"Who's this?" Palmer asked.

"Our new waitress. She's from the city."

"Swell. So my ear perks up, you know, 'cause this twerp of a kid is about to offer me a deal I can't refuse. He says he'll take five sacks of ice, but he's gonna store 'em in my freezer and just take a little bit at a time when he needs it. To pay for the ice, he's gonna mop my floor every night at closing, for five nights. Seemed like a good deal. So then I look out my window and see he's in business over here," Palmer said, frowning.

"Roast beef au jus?" suggested Stephanie.

"Naw, the usual," Palmer said. Stephanie shot me a frantic look.

I pulled her over by the cash register and whispered, "A bowl of chili and a small dinner salad with French dressing, and a Diet Coke."

"I'll have that ready for you in just a moment, sir," Stephanie said. Then she turned to me and hissed, "Where do I find the chili? Why aren't things clearly marked around here?"

"Who is that kid, anyway?" Palmer asked.

"He belongs to this guy, Cee Dubyah, who comes in a lot. Cee Dubyah left him here for a couple of days, I guess."

Johnny slammed a bowl of chili down on the pass-through, and I grabbed it up and rushed it to Palmer. "We serve the chili fast," I whispered to Stephanie, "before it cools down and the grease floats to the top."

Stephanie nodded, taking this fact in along with all the others that were going to make her a success in the restaurant business.

Before Palmer left, there were half a dozen other guys in, and a couple with a two-year-old kid — which translates into spoons and forks all over the floor, plus twenty crackers' worth of crumbs — so we were pretty busy and didn't think much about the fact that just about every guy who paid his bill bought a six-pack of beer, all different brands, on his way out.

As we found out later, they were stocking Tag's roadside beer stand. Lord only knows what kind of deal Tag had offered them.

Well, no self-respecting trucker drinks beer in the morning, so the next morning there was Tag at his stand, flogging newspapers. "*Wichita Eagle and Beacon,*" he sang out. "*Kansas City Star.* Cheaper than newsstand prices, right here."

Wise to this kid by now, I ran to the little newspaper boxes parked outside the door of the café. Sure enough, they were both empty.

"You pried open the boxes and stole our newspapers," I shouted.

"I didn't pry the stupid boxes open."

"Then how did you get the papers?" I asked with my arms folded across my chest like Mrs. Tideman, the P.E. teacher at my last school.

"I put in a quarter to get the box open, like any other customer," Tag explained. "I just borrowed the other newspapers, that's all. I'm paying you back."

"You little thief!"

48

"You don't have to get so worked up over a few crummy pieces of paper. It's just a temporary arrangement until my supply gets here."

"Your supply?"

"Well, yeah. I ordered a few dozen copies on consignment. They're delivering 'em to me about five thirty tomorrow morning. I told them what we had here was an untapped market. Who wants to pay those dumb newspaper box prices you charge?"

"I swear, I'm taking you to small claims court," I warned. "You're getting out of hand. When is Cee Dubyah coming back?"

Then this sort of shadow passed across Tag's face, and Stephanie nudged my arm. "He'll come back, don't you worry for a minute," Tag rasped. "But even if he didn't, I could get along just great. You know what? I'm going to be a thousandaire and then a millionaire and then a trillionaire before you even quit getting allowance from your mother. You watch."

"Omigosh," Stephanie squealed. "I swear, I'm going to write a book before this summer's over, and it's going to take place right here in Spinner, Kansas. I mean, what an exotic setting."

SIX

wwwwwwwwwwwwwwwwwwwwwwwwwwwwwwwwwwwwwwww

Tag had spent four nights in Red Cottage 4 without
a word from Cee Dubyah. Then, tucked in with the
Wichita paper on Sunday morning, there was a letter
Cee Dubyah must have left while we were all asleep.

> *Dear Whatsyernames at the Klondike Cafe,*
> *By now y'all see I've got my boy installed there*
> *at your place for a while. He's not going to be*
> *any trouble, because that Tag's a kid who knows*
> *what to do with himself. See that he gets a decent*
> *meal every day or two. He doesn't always think*
> *about things like that. He'll pay his own way,*
> *don't you worry.*
> *Listen, I am coming back, and I'll settle up with*
> *you on the room. I just can't make it yet. I'm*
> *asking y'all to trust me, just a while, hear?*
> *Tag got to you yet? It doesn't take that guy long,*
> *does it? I'll be seeing y'all as soon as I can swing*
> *it, all things considered.*
> *Take care.*
>
> *Gratefully,*
> *C. W. Layton*

Stephanie, Momma, and I sat in the empty cafe talking about whether to tell Tag we'd heard from Cee Dubyah.

"Maybe Cee Dubyah visited him last night," Stephanie suggested.

"Well, if he did Tag would never say a word about it," I reminded them. "He's the most stubborn, independent mule I ever saw."

"He has a right to know we've heard from his dad," Momma said.

"It would just make him sad, wouldn't it?" asked Stephanie. But then Stephanie is the kind of person who isn't happy unless she has at least twenty minutes of intense misery each day.

"But it'd be reassuring. At least he'd know Cee Dubyah is coming back, right?"

"Oh, sure, Aunt Marilyn, but *when*, he'll wonder. How long's the poor thing going to have to shift for himself?"

"Tag's no poor thing," I muttered. "He'll be opening a restaurant out there any day now."

"Let's show him the letter," Momma said.

"Let's lie about it," suggested Stephanie.

I had the only reasonable idea. "I say we look him over and see if he says anything about Cee Dubyah being here. If he does, we'll tell him about the letter. If he doesn't —"

"We'll tell him anyway," Momma said firmly.

"Who you talking about, that kid?" Johnny called out the pass-through. "Put him out on the highway. Maybe a truck'll run the runt over."

"Cook, Johnny. Don't philosophize," Momma said. "Oh dear, it is a responsibility having this child here. Your father will have a fit when he finds out."

"Oh, he'll pretend to have a fit, you know that, Momma, but he'll put up with it."

"Is he coming up this weekend, Aunt Marilyn?"

"Not until the end of the month," Momma said, shaking her head from side to side. "He's not terribly supportive about our efforts to feed the truckers, you know. He thinks we should settle down to respectable work. The last time we talked about it he suggested an insurance office . . ." Momma's voice trailed off.

I hid my face in my hands, bracing myself. Here it comes, I thought.

"Can you imagine anything more tedious than an insurance office? If there's anything I hate, girls, it's routine. Well, I'll just have to explain it all to Dad when he comes home next weekend. Or maybe Tag will be gone by then. See what you can do, Dovi. Johnny, what's our Sunday Special this week?"

"Squirrel," Johnny snarled.

"Oh, yuck!" cried Stephanie.

"You don't like squirrel? Then you can have chicken-fried and mashed potatoes," Johnny growled. "There isn't much I can do to hurt potatoes once they're smashed up that way, and a chicken-fried steak is a chicken-fried steak, even if I cook it in axle grease. Yep, squirrel's our Sunday Special, take it or leave it, folks."

"He's kidding," I whispered, for Stephanie had a squeamish stomach and was quite green. She couldn't even stand hearing someone talk about an operation while she was eating. When her face had turned back to its usual color I said, "Momma, we're going to look Tag over outside, and you can trust me to do what's best for him and us both, okay?"

"Oh, I know I can. You're just like your father, loaded with common sense. Thank goodness none of it rubbed off on me. You *will* tell him, however."

So, Stephanie and I went out looking for Tag at his roadside stand. In four days he'd gone from beer to beer and Life Savers to beer and Life Savers and newspapers. Then on Saturday he'd added a line of combs, disposable razors, and toothbrushes. I couldn't wait to see what he'd be selling on Sunday — maybe Bibles? But there was no sign of Tag out by the road.

"Do you think his father's come for him?" Stephanie asked.

"We just got the letter today. Maybe he's sick."

"We'd better go check his cabin, don't you think?"

Well, I knew Tag wasn't the kind of kid you just outright checked up on. "I've got a better idea. Let's go get a mop and stuff."

With a bucket of soapy water, some spray cans, a bunch of rags, and a bundle of clean sheets and towels we were armed to invade Tag's room. The calico curtains of Red Cottage 4 were pulled tight, as though they'd been pinned or paper-clipped together inside. And there was no light showing under the door, no sound of the radio or the air conditioner humming inside.

"Shall I knock?" asked Stephanie.

"How else is he going to know we're out here?" I replied lightly, but to tell the truth I was worried.

Stephanie knocked, pounded, beat on the door. I thought I heard someone scurrying around inside, like a puppy or something, but I couldn't be sure because a big semi was grinding its way out of our lot right behind the cottage.

"Use the key, for heaven's sake," Stephanie whispered.

On my belt loop was a jailer's ring, and I fumbled around for the key with the red dot painted on it. Stephanie pushed the door open while I was still wrestling the key out of the stubborn lock.

Believe me, the air in the room could have knocked out a pack of St. Bernards. It was a killer combination of sweat socks and overripe bananas. The room was pitch-dark besides; there wasn't a sliver of light. It took us awhile to spot Tag sitting in the middle of the bed and looking a lot like he was being stalked.

"Taggert!" I yelled.

"What are you doing in here?" he asked in a morning voice deeper than usual — a frightened voice, I thought, not the kind of angry sound I'd expect from a Tag cornered by two girls with a bucket of wash water.

"Well, we've got to clean the place," I huffed. "It smells like a pigsty. Can't you smell?"

Tag sniffed around like a bloodhound. "Smells just regular."

Stephanie coughed and busied herself dusting the rickety old desk.

"Hey, watch it, you," Tag warned. "I've got my business records over there."

"Sor-*ree*," Stephanie said.

"How come you're still in bed?" I asked. "You're missing customers. Half the guys have already pulled out for the day."

"Isn't it Sunday?" Tag scurried to the head of the bed and reached for something on the bedside table. It was too dark to see what he was fiddling with, but I guessed it was one of those nylon wallets, because there's no mistaking the grating sound of Velcro being yanked away from itself. Finally he pulled the chain on the bedside lamp, and yes, it was a wallet. He slid a card out to study under the dim light.

"Umhmm . . . like I said, it's Sunday. It says so right on my pocket calendar, so there, smarty."

"So what if it's Sunday?" Stephanie said. "You waiting for a ride to church?"

"It just so happens, I don't work on the Lord's day."

"Oh, pardon us. We didn't know you were such a saintly person. I mean, who would guess it of a guy who steals newspapers and sells beer against the laws of the state of Kansas. Would you have guessed it, Stephanie?"

"Never for a minute," she replied.

"Why are you guys so mean?" Tag asked.

Then I noticed that he was wrapping a towel around his middle and tying it in a messy knot at his left hip. "What's the towel for?"

"I don't have to tell you," Tag replied, inching under the sheet.

"Who cares, anyway?" I said. "All I know is we've got to clean out this hog pen or the county will condemn the whole Pig-Out, and then where are you going to go, huh?" Tag didn't answer, and in the dim light it seemed to me he got this worried look on his freckly face.

"She's just kidding. But we do have to clean, or none of the neighbors will be able to leave their windows open."

"What neighbors?" Tag taunted. "You never rent any of these holes out. Nobody would stay here who didn't have to."

"Oh, just get dressed," I said. "We'll be doing the bathroom."

"No," said Tag in this sorry little voice. "I can't."

"What do you think, we're going to look at you? You haven't got a thing we'd be interested in seeing." I shoved Stephanie toward the bathroom, wondering how we were both going to fit into that tiny slot while Tag got himself decent.

Oh, the bathroom! It smelled like a gym suit that'd been forgotten in the washing machine for a week, and it didn't take a minute to figure out why. Tag had strung a line from the shower head to a hook on the opposite wall, and flung over it were a pair of jeans, at least six used-to-be-white socks, two misshapen shirts, and three pairs of underpants. It was all wet, or damp, but no longer dripping into the puddle of water I'd just slipped around in. The underpants were drying into funny little twists of gray, like dishrags.

"Don't you have rules against things like this?" Stephanie asked. "He can't just do his laundry like this."

"Certainly not like *this*," I agreed, catching a whiff of the socks that were still black at the toes and pocked with little sticker stars from the wild grass out by Tag's roadside stand. By now my clogs had made a bunch of black smudges on the floor and I was squishing water between my toes, so I motioned to Stephanie that we should clear out.

Tag was in the bed, with the sheet pulled up to his head. One eye watched us.

I swallowed a lump in my throat, then said, "What do you think, Tag, that this isn't a first-class motel? Listen, we have laundry service here."

"Laundry service," Stephanie agreed. "Everybody just puts his clothes outside the door every day —"

"Every Sunday," I corrected her, "and the laundry staff does 'em up with the sheets and towels."

"Oh yeah? Nobody told us when me and Cee Dubyah checked in," said Tag, his voice muffled by the sheet.

"Oh sure," said Stephanie. "And guess what else. We provide loaner clothes while your stuff is being washed."

Loaner clothes? Where were we going to get anything to fit this shrimp? I gathered up all the grungy laundry from Tag's line, and we left the bucket and all in his room. "We'll be back in a while," I assured him.

"Next time knock," he shot back.

"Knock? We practically beat your door down," Stephanie reminded him.

"I wasn't ready for any company then. Later I might be. Depends."

"Oh, brother," I sighed, trying to hold Tag's smelly mess away from me so I wouldn't stink all day.

Stephanie said, "We've just got to get that child something to wear."

"Terrific, Stephanie. Got any ideas?"

"Johnny's old jeans?"

"In case you haven't noticed, Johnny weighs about four hundred pounds more than Tag, and even my dad's stuff would swim on him." I stepped back, like an artist admiring a model. "You're pretty slim, Steph. You haven't got a whole lot of shape," I added. "Have you got some old jeans we could make into cutoffs for Tag?"

"*Oh* no — I'm not sacrificing a perfectly good pair of jeans!" she protested. But it's no use trying to change my mind once it's set on something.

Half an hour later, with Tag's smelly heap soaking in Biz, we brought a decent pair of cutoffs down to Red Cottage 4 and knocked.

"Who is it?" came this sort of rasp from inside.

"Who do you think it is?"

Tag opened the door a crack, then backed up behind it so we could get in. I swear, the change in the room was amazing. He'd stripped the bed and tossed the dirty sheets into a corner, and the clean ones were tucked in as tight as a baby crib. All his "business papers" were stacked neatly on the desk, and we could see places on the floor where the mop water was drying in deformed shapes.

"Boy, you've been busy," I said. "Even wrapped in that stupid towel."

"Check the bathroom," he told us proudly. Sure enough, he'd Ajaxed the sink and tub to a glistening white, despite the cracks and rusted places, and the mirror over the sink, which he must have climbed on the toilet to reach, was sparkling and barely even smudgy. Except for a few hairs along the baseboard, the floor was spotless.

"Why, Tag, you're a regular houseboy," Stephanie cried.

"Am not!"

"Oh, shut up. That was a compliment, dope." I tossed him the jeans. "Here, get dressed."

He turned them this way and that. "Is this all?"

"It's hot out. You don't need a shirt or socks."

"He means the you-know-what's, Dov."

"Yeah, what am I s'posed to put on under these?"

"Nothing, macho man," I teased. "Oh well, these cutoffs are pretty soft and harmless, and we'll have your clothes disinfected in about a week, so don't worry."

He tightened the towel around his middle.

"Suit yourself," I shrugged. "If you ever get dressed, come on into the cafe for the Sunday Special. On Sundays we always feed our cottage customers for free. Especially if they're not wearing underwear."

SEVEN

〜〜〜〜〜〜〜〜〜〜〜〜〜〜〜〜〜〜〜〜〜〜〜〜〜〜〜〜〜〜〜

Stephanie had a major decision to make: was she going to stay at the Pig-Out for the summer to write her fiction novel, or was she going back to Wichita for Wayne Firestone's All Star game?

"This is a tough one, Dov. I — am — torn. I'd really like to stay and see how things turn out with Tag, and I wanted to finish my fiction novel, which I'm going to start tomorrow, but sometimes we have to make sacrifices for love."

By this time I'd heard so much about Wayne Firestone that I was beginning to believe he looked like one of those hulking gargoyles outside the Spinner Public Library, and I was sure he had as much personality as a head of iceberg lettuce.

"Look at it this way, Steph. Have you even gotten one letter, one single word from Wayne the whole time you've been here?"

"Well, no," Stephanie admitted. "But I promised him before I left that if he made the All Star team I'd be there for the game, and Judy wrote that he made it."

"I guess if he invited you . . ."

"Uh, well, he didn't exactly invite me. I sort of volunteered."

"Yeah, but if you're going with him . . ."

"We're not exactly going together. It's more like we're really good friends."

"Okay, so if you're so close . . ."

"Well, it's not exactly that we're terribly close — yet."

"Stephanie Fisher, what exactly is it between you and the great first baseman, Wayne Firestone?"

"You mean actually? Specifically?"

"I mean on the nose."

"The exact, particular, actual, specific nature of our relationship is that I'm wildly crazy about Wayne Firestone, and he's wildly crazy about baseball."

"He doesn't even like girls?"

"Baseball, and Emily Ryan," Stephanie said miserably.

"Oh, Steph." I put my arms around her, feeling genuinely sorry for her. But deep inside my heart was pounding joyfully because Stephanie hadn't really gotten any further than I had in the boyfriend department.

"Emily Ryan is four foot eleven," Stephanie said, "and she has red hair that she wears in a wedge that bounces."

"Oh no, the worst — bouncy hair," I cried, yanking on the brown straw that hung to my shoulders.

"She's what my mother calls 'perky,'" Stephanie confessed. "Perky, bouncy, they go hand in hand. And her hair's not the only thing that bounces. It makes me positively nauseous."

I handed her a carry-out sack. "Here, have a barf bag."

She grabbed one of the cheap, bristly napkins we kept in the holders — I mean, these napkins could scrape off the top layer of flesh — and she wiped the tears off her face. Blush and dripping mascara went with the tears. "On the other hand, if I'm not there for the All Star game, Emily could really get a stranglehold, and Wayne will be lost forever." This was enough to soak two more napkins. I pulled out a stack as thick as a Viva sponge.

"Wayne Firestone sinks into the bog." I pronounced

it as if I were reading an *Eagle and Beacon* headline. "Starting first baseman's head visible only for seconds before he is sucked into the gurgling mud. Implicated in the drowning is fifteen-year-old Emily Ryan, described by classmates as perky. Wayne Firestone is survived by Stephanie Fisher, waitress at the world famous Pig-Out Inn of Spinner, Kansas."

Stephanie giggled and sort of brightened a bit, with her face all streaked in about three different shades. "This is really dumb, isn't it?"

"Yeah, really dumb."

"But I'm part of a long tradition. Cleopatra and Juliet and all."

"They're dead. I'm not sure, were they ever really people?"

"Oh yes. I went to Shakespeare-in-the-Park last summer and saw at least one of them, I forget which. Anyway, if they weren't real, they should have been."

As far as I was concerned the whole issue of Stephanie's leaving was decided right then and there, but I guess she wasn't sure until the next Saturday, when something happened to convince her.

The Army came for its usual weekly siege. There were only eighteen of them this time wanting cheeseburgers and fries and shakes on the double. But one of them was destined to be the new Wayne Firestone.

Oh, I'd come far since the first invasion. I could carry plates of cheeseburgers all the way up my arm, four at a time, and I could do milkshakes without needing to be hosed down afterwards. Stephanie was no help at all, though. She latched on to the youngest guy in the group and delivered one-on-one waitress service. He got his order first, of course, and then she surrounded his burger plate with a whole detail of regular mustard, hot mustard, ketchup, barbecue sauce, and steak sauce. I came by to grab a couple of the bottles for the other customers and recognized this guy, mostly because he seemed so young and so unmilitary, sitting on a stool two away from the nearest soldier. "You're the guy who left the retainer a few weeks ago, aren't you?" I asked. It was funny to see the kid blush almost purple. "I've got it under here somewhere. I stuck it in a cottage cheese container." I groped around under the counter.

"Oh, it's okay. I don't need it anymore. The orthodontist says I'm good as done." He pulled his lips back and showed us his new, improved bite, like a cocker spaniel's. Stephanie was awed. I thought, here's a guy she could really sink her teeth into.

I flew around the cafe, taking care of all the customers and making snide remarks at Stephanie. "If it's not too much trouble, cut the apple pie, will you?" and

66

"Never hire a waitress from the city if you expect the coffeepot to stay filled." She paid no attention because she was zeroing in on the guy, who turned out to be a buck private in basic training named Eddie Perini. I overheard scraps of their conversation as I dashed around attending to the guys who were already on seconds and thirds.

"How come you're in the Army?" I heard her ask, and I leaned over to catch the answer.

Eddie turned his pockets inside out. "No money for college," he said. "Uncle Sam will put me through."

About six cheeseburgers later I heard, "Do you play baseball, Eddie?"

"Do I play baseball!" I glanced over and saw him eating his milkshake with a fork. Stephanie must have put in about nine scoops of ice cream.

The last thing I caught was Eddie asking her if she'd lived in Spinner long, and her replying that she'd just moved there, and him saying he hoped she'd be staying a long time, and her saying, well, she was still in high school, so it looked like she had a few years to go, and him saying, well, he'd be finishing up his radio training in a couple of weeks, and he didn't know where he'd be shipped, and her saying she was thinking of moving back to Wichita at the end of the summer anyway.

Boy, I had a lot to learn about male-female give-

and-take. From the juke box, Elvis pleaded Eddie's case: "Love me tender, love me true."

Then Tag came in, wearing Stephanie's cutoffs and his alligator shirt. He climbed onto the stool next to Eddie's.

"I might join the Army," he said.

A guy down at the end of the counter said, "Don't say it too loud. They'll sign you up."

"Maybe the Air Force is better," said Tag.

"Anything's better," one of the soldiers said with a laugh. Only Eddie seemed to be taking Tag seriously.

"What do you want with the Army?" he asked.

Tag shrugged. "Travel."

"So far I've been to Kansas," Eddie said, "which is where I started from."

"A place to lay your head at night," Tag said.

"Just don't sign up too early," Eddie warned him. "You want your hair cut short like this?" He pulled Tag's hand up to feel the stubble at the back of his head. "You want to take a shower every day? You want to mop floors and make your bed at five thirty every morning?"

Tag looked confused. "Is that all there is to it?"

"Naw, that's just the good stuff," one of the soldiers laughed.

"Well, I haven't made up my mind yet."

"You got time," said Eddie, offering Tag some of his fries.

"Hey, listen, guys," Tag said, "any of you need a shoe shine? I've got my kit outside. Drop by after lunch. That's one thing you won't have to do back at the base. Just bring me all your shoes. I work cheap, and I don't just use spit, either."

"He uses real polish, man!" one guy said, taking off his shoes. "Here, do mine!"

Tag shook his head. "Sorry, I'm on my lunch hour."

Tag adopted a dog — unless he traded somebody's grandmother for it. I was afraid to ask. The scruffy-looking mongrel slept in the shade next to Tag's road-side stand/shoe shine parlor and ate candy bars with Tag. I don't know where he slept at night, but I have an idea.

"What's your friend's name?" I asked, heading to Yellow Cabin 6 after the lunch rush one day.

"Fenway," he said.

"What kind of a ridiculous name is Fenway?"

"He's named after my favorite ballpark, over there in Boston, Massachusetts."

"Have you ever been to Boston?" I asked.

"Me and Cee Dubyah are going there for a baseball game. Maybe next summer."

"Tag, when do you figure Cee Dubyah's coming back?"

"It won't be long," he said.

"It's already been long."

"So? You don't have a father, what do you know?"

"I do too have a father. He's coming home Friday. You'll meet him. By the way, I was wondering, where's your mother?"

"I'm not supposed to answer that," Tag said softly.

"How come you're not living with her?"

"You're the nosiest girl I ever met," said Tag, waving to a trucker who was pulling in for a late-afternoon breather. Fenway raised his lazy head for a second to bark absently at the driver, then settled back into his coil at Tag's feet.

"You going to be out here long?" I asked.

"Until the sun goes down. By then everybody's in for the night."

"Oh. Well, see you later." Now was my opportunity. Stephanie was taking a nap and Tag was peddling, so I grabbed the keys from the hook in the kitchen and stole over to Tag's cottage. I'd made a couple of attempts to find Cee Dubyah's note, but Tag had done

one thorough job of hiding it — or maybe he carried it with him all the time.

Tag's cottage was looking pretty good; he'd probably have done all right in an Army barracks. I rummaged through the papers and comic books on Tag's desk; even found odd dollars between the pages of a *Sports Illustrated,* and about seventy-five dollars more scattered around in his drawers, which were mostly empty. No sign of the note. It was deadly hot in the room. I thought I'd do Tag a favor and turn on the air conditioning so he could come back to a cool cabin when he was through work. Flipping open the control box of the window unit, I found it — Cee Dubyah's note folded into a tiny square.

> *Dear Tag, my boy,*
>   *I got to do this, so we can be together someday. You and me are like two peas in a pod, and she's got no business keeping us apart.*
>   *Listen, I checked these people out real good, and they're okay. They're Quakers. Did ya ever read in school about the Quakers who kept the escaped slaves, so no one could find them? They'll watch out for you. But you understand I have to stay away, because the cops'll be looking for me until this all blows over and she forgets all about it.*
>   *You're just like a cat who jumps out of a tree and lands on his feet every time. You'll do all*

right, son. Here's a few dollars to start your
business with. I'll be back to get you as soon as
I can. I swear, we're going to Fenway Park before
the summer's out.

Your dad,
C.W.

I folded the letter back up the way it was. I wished
I hadn't found it. My chest felt tight and sore because
the letter was so sad, and I was disgusted with myself
for invading what little bit of privacy Tag had. Once,
when we were in our *Doctor Zhivago* stage, Stephanie
and I found some love letters my father and mother
had written back and forth, and we devoured the first
two, giggling and practically panting through every
line. But I felt sort of sick afterwards, and I never
admitted to Momma that I even knew where the letters were stored. Momma and Dad never looked quite
the same to me after that. I wondered if I was going
to be able to treat Tag just the same. The last thing I
wanted was to feel sorry for the kid, but even with the
air conditioner blowing in my face at full blast I
couldn't shake the hot heavy feeling of sadness that
gripped my chest.

I knew I wouldn't be able to tell Stephanie about the
letter. She'd always lived in a regular three-bedroom,
two-story house with her mother and father and two
brothers, and there were very old apple trees in the

yard, and they'd never once had to submit a change-of-address card at the Post Office. She wouldn't understand about the Laytons of the world.

I turned off the air conditioner and put the note, folded no bigger than a postage stamp, back where I'd found it.

EIGHT

〜〜〜〜〜〜〜〜〜〜〜〜〜〜〜〜〜〜〜〜〜〜〜〜〜〜〜〜〜〜

"Your father wrote us a letter," Momma said as Tag slurped up a bowl full of sweet cereal milk, spoon by spoon. He didn't even look up, but Stephanie and I could tell he was listening by the way his shoulders grew stiff and alert.

Momma continued, "He says he'll get back just as soon as he can."

"We're supposed to look after you," I added.

"Did he say that?" Tag asked Momma.

"Well, not in so many words."

"Thought so." He slumped back over his cereal bowl. He held his spoon with his whole hand folded over it the way every kid does, the way I used to until Momma said it was unladylike, with gorgeous hands like mine, and she taught me to hold a fork just like a pencil. Tag kept up a steady rhythm with the spoon and never lost a drop of the milk. You didn't even have to wipe the counter after Tag was done eating.

Stephanie munched one of Johnny's lead biscuits, gold-soaked with honey, and said, "Your dad thought you'd grow on us."

"I'm growing, I'm growing," Tag said with a faint smile into his cereal bowl.

"You're growing, all right. You're growing rich," I yelled.

By now his bowl was bone-dry, and he'd eaten his toast down to thin little V's of crust and had a tomato juice moustache. He jumped down from the stool. "Put it on my tab."

"Yes, sir," I said, saluting. But subtlety was lost on Tag, because now his mind was strictly on business. He effortlessly hoisted a carton of goods onto his shoulder and backed out the door. It was the perfect time to set up shop; the sun was still way behind the building, and there was a fifty-fifty chance for a decent breeze until about noon.

Stephanie curled into the sunniest booth with her notebook open on the table and six freshly sharpened pencils stacked like Lincoln Logs in front of her. She was on page one of her fiction novel, she said, but it looked more like she was staring into thin air and scratching mosquito bites a lot.

Out in back I heard the water going as Johnny chased the wind-blown dirt away from our door with the hose. Momma was back in her cottage washing her hair, and she was going to sit with her feet up on a hassock and let her hair.dry naturally while she read one of her library books.

"If anybody comes in, you're going to have to cook," I warned Stephanie.

"Shhh, I'm thinking hard." She was also chewing hard, chewing on ice, and the crunch-crunch, plus the thought of that freezing feeling on my teeth, was starting to get to me.

"Wait, wait, it's coming to me." Stephanie had this dreamy look washing over her. Even her wrists went limp, kind of like the androids you see on Star Trek reruns that get messages inside their heads. "Listen to my opening sentence, and tell me honestly, is — it — not — great? 'On a sun-blistered afternoon deep in picturesque suburban — no, *rural* — Kansas, a desperately handsome and sinewy Army lieutenant named Ernie Polini — is that too close to his real name? — named Andy Marini walked through the door of an oasis on the prairie to behold the face of the — no, of *his* one true destined love, Honorée.' That — is — a — grabber! What do you think, Dov?"

I wasn't thinking. What I was doing was watching this highway patrol car pull into our lot. Two officers rolled down their windows and got out of the car. I could hear the cracking, fuzzy sound of the police radio, clearer now that the officers were opening our door.

"Morning, ladies. Mind if we leave this open a wedge so we can catch the dispatcher?"

Stephanie flipped her notebook shut, as if the policemen cared one bit about her corny story, and she dashed over next to me and started stuffing napkins into the smudgy metal holders.

The officers ordered a couple of Dr. Peppers.

"Do we charge them?" Stephanie whispered hot in my ear.

"Of course. You think we're bribing the police?" I replied as I stuck two sweet rolls in the microwave. Half a minute later the pats of butter had melted all over the sweet rolls, and I gave one to each of the patrolmen. "On the house," I said. Stephanie rolled her eyes toward the ceiling.

"Whose place is this?" asked Officer Somebody — Bodeker, his name tag said.

"Mine. I mean my parents'." I was suddenly very sweaty under the arms; I knew what they wanted.

"Do you sell Coors here?" the other officer, whose name was Geary, asked casually.

"Well, I don't actually sell it myself."

"Me either," Stephanie quickly added.

"You see, my mother's here all the time." Of course, she was nowhere in sight, and I knew, now that the hose was off, that Johnny would be out back on a lettuce crate, smoking a cigar and reading the *National Enquirer*, before he had to get lunch going. "Anyway, I know you guys were only kidding me, because a Kansas highway patrolman wouldn't drink even a drop while he was on duty, right?"

The two officers laughed and drew on their Dr. Pepper straws awhile. Finally Bodeker said, "We'd like to ask you a few questions, ladies. You know a guy name C. W. Layton?"

I stayed cool, of course, but Stephanie dropped the box of napkins, and they snowed all over the floor.

"Oh, sure," I said. "He's a big burly truck driver who stops by here from time to time. I think he drives out of Denver. That, or St. Louis, I'm not sure which."

"Has he been in today?" asked Geary.

"No, sir."

"When was the last time he was here?"

"Cee Dubyah?" I knew the day, even the hour, but

I dallied, scratching my head. "Well now, let's see. Stephanie's been here a couple of weeks, and it seems like — you've never met Cee Dubyah, have you, Steph?"

"Never once, in my whole life, I swear," she swore.

"So he must not have been in here for about two weeks. Fifteen, sixteen days, maybe."

Bodeker asked, "Was there anybody with him?"

"You mean, did he have anybody with him, like when he left here last time?" I asked.

"I mean, was there a kid with him?"

"I don't *think* he was hauling goats," I replied sweetly.

"A child, a boy," Geary explained, patiently. "About eight or ten years old."

Well now, I knew for a fact that Tag *was* exactly nine, so I could easily say without lying, "No, no boy eight or ten came in here with Cee Dubyah." Stephanie flashed me an admiring smile. I practically twisted my neck out of its socket, checking to be sure Tag wasn't out there making a liar of me. Nothing was out there — not his orange-crate roadside stand, not Fenway, not a clue that Taggert Layton had even been alive, let alone living at the Pig-Out Inn.

"We get a lot of guys from Fort Riley in here," I added, "but the youngest one is probably eighteen."

79

Stephanie was shaking her head *No! No!* as if I were turning her baby doll Eddie over to the cops.

"We're interested in a child traveling with Layton," Geary said firmly.

And again I could answer honestly, "Aw, there's no boy traveling with Cee Dubyah."

Stephanie moved in closer. "What's Cee Dubyah done, something illegally criminal?" she asked.

"Just some mess over in Wichita, and they're having us check on him up and down the road. Nothing for you to worry about, ladies."

"Nothing, nothing at all," Officer Geary assured us, sucking air at the bottom of his glass. Then he pulled a small school picture out from behind his identification card, and there Tag lay on our counter, looking shined up and greased down in a blue striped button-down shirt and a denim vest. I could imagine his mother fussing over him that morning, getting every hair in place, and tucking his shirt in just so, and making sure breakfast didn't show anywhere on his freckly face.

"If this kid turns up with Layton, you let us know, hear?" Bodeker said, and he made it sound like a threat. He wrote the Kansas highway patrol number down on a napkin, which I was sure I'd lose soon. Then he handed me a couple of dollars for the Dr. Peppers and sweet rolls. "Keep the change."

"Just who's doing the bribing?" I whispered to Stephanie as we heard their car doors slam.

"I swear, I've held my breath for the last twelve minutes," Stephanie said, gasping like a sprinter. "Why exactly are they looking for Cee Dubyah? Did he steal something, or is he a smuggler, or a Russian spy?"

No, I didn't think he was a smuggler or a spy. What I thought, way in the back of my mind, was that Cee Dubyah was some kind of kidnapper — only Tag wanted, with all his heart, to be kidnapped.

In a little while Fenway came strolling out and plopped down in his sleepy spot, and then Tag came out and got his shop set up as quickly as an umbrella snapping up, or a carnival tent over in the Safeway parking lot.

I left Stephanie waiting on a P.I.E. trucker who wanted scrambled eggs, grits, hash browns — the whole works — and went out to check on Tag.

"Lay low," I warned the shrimp. "They've got a picture of you."

"Which one?"

"Aw, some crummy school picture. Your hair's plastered down."

Tag nodded, twirling his Cokes around in the ice. He was using one of Johnny's huge pots as an ice bucket.

"So what are you going to do, just stand out here on a public highway? You might as well flag the cops down next time they drive by, in case they happen to miss you."

"You are really stupid, Dovi."

"Stupid!"

"Didn't I disappear when those cops showed up?"

"Well, yes."

"But now I've got to get back to work."

"Oh, come on! What if they come back?"

"You don't know anything about the free enterprise system."

"Yeah, and you're a graduate of the Harvard Business School, right?"

"I am a graduate of the school of hard knocks," Tag said. I swear, I could have closed my eyes and heard Cee Dubyah talking.

"Which means?"

"Which means, business is business. If a guy needs something and another guy has it to sell, you got business. You got business, you got profit. Then you buy more stuff with the profit, and you sell more stuff. Then you take the extra profit and you buy stuff you need for yourself, like cheeseburgers and toothpaste. There isn't one other thing you have to know about business," he said, and then his whole tone changed as some trucker came over to check out the shop. Fenway got so excited that he all but knocked over Tag's orange-crate pyramid.

"Good morning, sir." Tag dripped charm. "Heading out, or home?"

"I'm heading back to Kansas City for a few days of R and R with the wife and kids. What have you got here?"

"I've got all kinds of cold drinks, but it's too early for beer."

"A kid like you selling beer?" the driver said, and I could see him holding in a great big laugh.

"Oh, no, sir," Tag said, as if he were good and shocked at the very idea. "The beer's one hundred percent absolutely free." He waited till the trucker's eyebrows raised up high, then added, "But I charge a dollar for the paper cup."

"Well, I believe I'll buy me one of your paper cups, then," the trucker said.

"No sale," Tag told him, crossing his arms stubbornly across his chest. "How am I going to sleep tonight if you wreck between here and K.C. 'cause you're drunk on my beer?"

"One lousy beer?"

"Okay, picture this," Tag said in that style I'd come to know so well, where he drew pictures in the air. "You're riding along, and you start to doze off." His hands showed us the path of the truck, drunkenly snaking down the highway. "Suddenly you wake up to a siren blasting in your ears." There were full sound effects, with Fenway barking the way any respectable dog would bark at a fire truck. "A cop pulls you over, and he smells beer on your breath. So you tell him, 'Gosh, officer, all I did was buy a paper cup from a kid eighty miles back,' and bingo! We both spend a night in the slammer."

"It's not a pretty picture," the trucker said, staring into Tag's thin air.

"But, I'll give you an ice cold Coke for free."

"How much for the cup?"

"Free."

"What's your angle?"

"You got anything in your cab for the kids at home?"

The trucker glanced over at his truck and back at Tag with a guilty look on his face. "Naw, I'm only away half of every week. It's no big deal when I come home."

"You're going home to those sweet babies empty-handed?" Tag asked, as if he were personally offended. " 'You didn't bring me nothing, Daddy? Again?' "

Well, that trucker headed back to his rig with his free Coke and about fifteen dollars' worth of absolute junk — carnival prizes like spider rings and Chinese finger-prisons.

Tag flicked a refreshing shower of water from the ice bucket on Fenway, who barked and nuzzled his nose gratefully in Tag's crotch.

I stepped back for a second to watch the two of them, especially the twerp of a kid in his high-water jeans and baggy alligator shirt, and I realized I was in the presence of a genuine pro.

"That was too simple, Fenway," Tag said. "What an easy mark."

NINE

Barbara and Bill Wanamaker came in for some lemonade. Barbara dipped her pinkie into the glass and let the baby suck on it. She was getting bigger and bigger and wouldn't be willing to hang around in that serving tray much longer, so the Wanamakers were spelling each other through the night, not even stopping to catch a few hours in a bed.

While we all clucked over the baby a truck driver came in who just wasn't like the others. Most of the customers would say "Cuppa java, black," or "Gimme two scrambled." This guy looked like the rest in faded jeans that sagged at the knees and seat and an AH, KANSAS! T-shirt, but as soon as he opened his mouth we knew he was different.

"Would you be kind enough to bring me a piping hot cup of creamed coffee, with a warm scone at the side?" The Wanamakers glanced at each other and snickered, and even the baby smiled, but the Gentleman never noticed. He had his face buried in a red magazine that had no picture on the cover, just small white letters. The only words I caught were *Journal of*.

Tag was mopping up his fried eggs with a wedge of toast. "What's a scone?" he asked me.

"Oh, a scone, well. It's a . . . it's like a sausage . . . not links of course, but a sausage pattie, about so big around." I made a circle with my fingers, starting at about watermelon size and working down to something that would fit alongside a cup of coffee.

"I don't believe you for a minute. The guy said he wanted it warm. People eat sausage sizzling hot," Tag said.

"What he meant was warmish hot. Nothing's ever served hot around here, you know that. A warmish hot, used-to-be sizzling sausage."

In the back booth, Stephanie smoothed a page of her notebook and said, "You are both utter fools. Don't you know that a scone is a tropical fruit? It's related to the papaya and the mango, only not as fleshy.

Mango! That's what I'll call the mynah bird in my fiction novel. And I'll call the Malaysian houseboy Papaya. Brilliant, Stephanie, brilliant."

"You have a Malaysian houseboy in your story in Kansas?" Just where did Stephanie think we were?

"My fiction novel is populated with very sophisticated people who've been around, Dovi. But you wouldn't know, because you don't read. Oh, of course you *read*, but you only read true crime and things like that. Not the realistic world of romance, the world of mynah birds and scones."

The Gentleman lowered the *Journal of* a couple of inches. "For those who are interested, a scone is a flat cake, similar to, but flatter than, a muffin, and not as sweet."

Okay, I was a little off on this one — but not as far off as Stephanie. Still, it stung just a little. "I don't think we've got anything on our menu like that," I said hotly.

"An English muffin will do. You have English muffins?"

"Nope."

"A biscuit, perhaps?" His eyes were teasing.

"I can give you a biscuit, but it'll be like a hockey puck."

"Allow me to revise my order. One cup of creamed coffee, steaming hot, and one warm hockey puck."

"Mister, are you from London, England?" Tag asked.

"No, but I'm an English teacher. I *was* an English teacher."

"An English teacher!" Stephanie jumped up and slammed her notebook shut. "It just so happens that I'm writing a fiction novel."

"Remarkable," the Gentleman said.

"I could show you some of the best parts of it," Stephanie generously offered.

"Very brave of you," he replied, "but I couldn't accept the compliment."

"Sure you could. Here, just read the smashing opening sentence." She slid the notebook in front of his *Journal of* and waited eagerly.

His eyes flew over the notebook, and he gently put it down. He took a bite of the hockey puck. "I haul meat and fresh produce and milk," he said. "I don't critique papers."

"Oh, I understand fully," Stephanie gushed. "But just let me read it to you, for the full dramatic impact. 'On a sun-blistered afternoon deep in picturesque rural Kansas, a desperately handsome and sinewy

Army lieutenant named Andy Marini walked through the door of an oasis on the prairie to behold the face of his one true destined love, Honorée.' Well? What do you think?"

The Gentleman responded, "I'm not paid to think. Just to drive."

"But what *do* you think?" I insisted.

"Honestly?"

"Absolutely honestly," Stephanie assured him. She whispered aside to Tag and me, "I always get A's in English."

"Responding strictly as a sophomore English teacher, I would say your spelling, punctuation, and sentence structure are excellent."

"See?" Stephanie said, practically spreading her plumes.

"Responding as a creative writing teacher, I would say your opening sentence is . . ." He sighed deeply.

"Go ahead, tell her!" I urged him.

"Trite."

"What does trite mean?" asked Stephanie, not sure just what kind of compliment this was.

"Ordinary. Predictable. Overblown." There was a small gasp from Stephanie, and he added hastily, "But I haven't come to the part about the Malaysian houseboy yet, or the mynah named Mango. That's

surely where your story begins to sparkle with orig-
inality."

"Yes," Stephanie said, backing away with her notebook. "That's a definite high point."

The Gentleman said, "I urge you to keep writing.
It's an excellent romantic outlet for a girl of your ob-
vious . . . sensitivity."

"Oh no, you've encouraged her," I groaned, for now
Stephanie's pencil raced over the pages of the notebook and I knew I wouldn't get a stick of work out of
her for the rest of the morning.

"So how come you're not teaching school?" Tag
asked in that way he had of piercing right through to
your gut. Come to think of it, my way.

The Gentleman reached for his wallet and spread
three pictures on the counter, all bald babies dressed
in uncomfortable red clothes, and piled like a pyramid.
"Twins, almost two years old, and a new baby," he
explained. "I can't feed them on what a teacher makes."

"Maybe you have too many kids," Tag said.

"Oh no. I have too many wives. My first one has
two children, teenagers. This is my second wife." He
handed us a picture of a dumpy little woman who
looked like a "before" ad for a weight-reducing pill.

"Listen to this," Stephanie cried. "Listen — to —
this! 'Mango and Papaya were inseparable. Bird and

man as one, until Papaya's employer, the lovely and desirable Honorée, sold the mynah bird to a passing truck driver. Papaya wept three days and three nights on his grass mat, until Honorée's young heart was breaking for the short, weeping Malaysian houseboy, so she made the truck driver give Papaya the bird. Meanwhile, Andy Marini —' "

"Wait, wait. Don't give the whole plot away," the Gentleman said, gulping the last of his coffee. He plunked some coins down under his saucer. "Well, thank you, boys and girls, and especially you over there, with the pencil. You've convinced me that I'm much better off driving a truck than teaching English."

That night Stephanie, Tag, and I were lined up on stools at the counter like See, Hear, and Speak No Evil. Stephanie was scribbling away in her notebook; the scratching pencil was the only noise in the place except for the buzzing of an overhead fan that badly needed oiling and the sound of our straws sucking up root beer floats.

After listening to the air for a long time I asked Tag, "Did you ever consider writing a book?"

"I haven't got anything to write about."

"Not true. You could write a book called, um, *How to Make Your First Million Before You're Twelve.*"

"I've got plenty of business ideas," Tag admitted, moving his eyes around the room as if he were reading ideas off the wall.

Stephanie looked up from her notebook to catch a sip of her root beer float. "I started writing when I was even younger than you," she bragged. "As a child, I was writing poetry that rhymed."

"My mother had a poem in a magazine once," Tag revealed.

As far as I could remember this was the first time he'd ever mentioned his mother, and I wasn't about to let it pass. "Well, why don't we write to your mother and ask her to send you a copy, for inspiration on your millionaire book? Where does she live?"

"I told you, I'm not supposed to say."

"I'm not going to tell anybody," I protested. "I just want to know for your own good."

"You're sticking your nose in again where it doesn't belong," Tag said snidely.

"Well, I'm not dumb, you know. I can go to the Spinner Public Library and look up all the Laytons in the Wichita telephone book, and I'd find her after a while."

"She has a different last name," Tag said quietly.

"How could that be?" asked Stephanie, chewing on her eraser.

"Figure it out." Tag's face revealed nothing.

I considered the possibilities. One, Tag's mother and father had never been married to each other. Two, they were married, and his mother had kept her own name; but that didn't seem like the kind of thing a man like Cee Dubyah would allow. Three, they were married, but she'd taken back her own name after they were divorced — but did that make sense if she had a child? And four, she'd remarried after her divorce. "Tag, has your mother got a new husband?"

"What do you mean by 'new'?" he asked.

"So that's it! You hate your stepfather," Stephanie cried. "That's why you don't want to live with your mother."

Tag spun around on his stool and glared at Stephanie. "I don't hate him. I just like my dad better."

The fan whirred and squeaked; we didn't know what to say. Finally Tag jumped into the silence. "I won't make my first million before I'm twelve anyway. I guess I won't write the book."

TEN

~~~~~~

Johnny brought my dad in from the bus station at about seven thirty Friday night. We all could have gone, Tag and Fenway and everybody, if all personnel under the age of sixteen had been willing to ride in the back of Johnny's pick-up. But Stephanie was afraid she'd get a hair out of place. And she didn't want road dust glopping onto her make-up.

So we decided to close the Pig-Out early and have a surprise party for Dad when he got home. Everything was as black as a skillet. We set Fenway up as our look-out. As soon as he spotted Johnny's pick-up turning into the lot, he started hollering, which was our signal to flip on the neon sign and all the lights and the juke box. The whole place was shimmering when Dad and Johnny walked in.

"Mike, Mike!" Momma threw her arms around his

waist and smothered him with little kisses up and down his face.

"I can't even breathe. Give me a chance to breathe, Marilyn. Dovi!" Dad stretched his arms out to me and included Stephanie in his hug, and we looked a sight — one tall, bearded, half-bald man with three women plastered to him.

Then he noticed Tag sitting alone in the last booth. "Well, who's this?" Dad asked.

"Some waif, name's Tag," Johnny replied. "Lives here, eats like a horse."

Dad looked confused, but Momma flashed him one of her I'll-explain-later looks, which he was used to, because Momma always had something outlandish to explain later.

"How was your bus ride, Uncle Mike?" Stephanie asked when we'd finally all crammed ourselves into a booth.

"It was the slowest trip on record. Do you know how many cow town stops there are between Wichita and Spinner?"

"Thirty-seven?" Momma guessed, and Dad growled. Momma was always doing that. Dad would try to impress us with how many, how tall, how old, how heavy, and how much–type questions, and Momma would always guess way over the normal, expected maximum.

To Dad, the computer man, the world was precise and had at least some rules and logical limits. To Momma, the 93,000,000 miles from Earth to the sun wasn't much farther than the 240,000 miles from Earth to the moon, because both were a long way off, and both looked about the same distance to the naked eye, and anyway she had no plans to visit either one. Momma was much more concerned about whether domestic workers, maids and all, were unionized and got decent benefits, or about prayer in the schools (against) and increasing voter registration in the South (for), or about how many scoops of ice cream you could get from a gallon drum. So she guessed, "Thirty-seven?" and Dad growled.

"Nine," he said, "and at some of the stops nobody even got on or off."

"Oh well, hey, the only one getting off at Spinner was this guy here," Johnny said. "The bus slowed down to just about twenty and shoved him off."

"Yeah, Johnny caught me as I fell out the door with my suitcase."

I thought of a million things to tell him and couldn't figure out where to start. Then he patted Tag's head in that sweet poppa way he had and said, "So, how are you doing, Tag?"

"Okay."

"He's doing a lot better than okay," I reported. "He's in business for himself. He believes in the free enterprise system," I said, with a little hoot.

"A tycoon, huh?" Dad said.

"Sir?"

"A hot-shot businessman. What kind of business are you in, Tag?"

"Oh, five-and-dime, cold drinks, newspapers, shoe shine." I half expected Tag to pull out a printed card.

"Say, is your house near here?"

Tag motioned with a flip of his mop to some dark place out there.

"Are your parents long-time Spinner people?"

Momma gave Dad such a kick under the table that we felt it all the way down the line. Across the booth, Stephanie jumped about a foot.

Johnny'd made us an apple pie for the party. Well, sort of an apple pie. It was a big oblong thing full of hot crunchy sliced apples, with a two-inch layer of his killer biscuit dough on top. It wasn't as bad as it sounds, with chocolate ice cream melting over the top and dribbling into the apples.

But while Johnny hacked up the pie with a butcher knife and Momma scooped ice cream, Tag tried to slip out on us.

"Hey, where are you going?" I demanded.

"Home," the twerp said in a small, puppy-dog voice.

"No, you don't!"

Momma went over and put her arm around him. Never mind that chocolate ice cream was dripping down his Red Sox shirt. "Please stay, Tag."

He shook his head.

"Why not?" Momma asked.

"Because I pay my own way."

"But it's a party," said Stephanie, who didn't seem to have any problem mooching off us for the summer.

Again, Tag shook his rag-mop head. "I pay my own way," he repeated. "And I don't feel like paying for a piece of Johnny's apple pie!"

Johnny howled and slapped his knee, and we all had a good laugh, and after a little while Johnny slipped out to see Tag safely back to Red Cottage 4.

Luckily for Dad, we didn't get the whole U.S. Army on Saturday morning. Just Eddie Perini, with the perfect teeth, who spent about two hours in a back booth with Stephanie because Momma and Dad wouldn't let her go anywhere with him.

Every so often I'd look over, and they'd be arm-wrestling and sneaking smooches and looking lovesick. Most of the time we all tried to ignore them, except when Momma brought them frosty mugs of root beer overflowing with foam.

Dad hadn't got the hang of the restaurant business. He tried to help during the lunch-hour rush, but he was too big for our narrow work space. It was like bumper cars. "Dad, hand me the mayo," I barked at him when the Pig-Out was full of truckers hungry for a quick lunch.

"The mayo, the mayo," he said, looking around like a kid at the state fair.

"Mayo-*nnaise*," I reminded him, and I pointed to the jar with my head, since my arms were loaded clear to the elbows with plates of food. Then Momma came tearing out of the kitchen, kicking the swinging door ahead of her, while Johnny slammed a plate of loose spaghetti on the pass-through. Dad was pinned between the swinging door and the pass-through, with one hand stuck in the ice maker, as spaghetti sauce flew all over his shirt.

"Oh, Mike, I'm sorry," Momma cried, rubbing his half-frozen paw with a warm towel, which we'd just used to mop up a cup of hot chocolate. Momma turned Dad around, the way you turn kids for Pin-the-Tail-on-the-Donkey, and pushed him by the waist to the booth with the big hole in the upholstery where no one ever sat. "Here are the receipts, Mike." She patted the solar-operated calculator in his shirt pocket. "Have fun!" she said, and then she got away quickly. Although Momma carefully kept the month's bills and receipts in a cigar box, she never added anything up.

"Marilyn Chandler, how can you run a business this way?" Dad groaned.

Momma yelled back over the lunch counter, "Oh, you know me. I'm the creative force behind it all, but you, you're the cool-headed businessman." All the truckers knew she was flattering him outrageously, and they loved every minute of it. Stephanie and I had the feeling that our regulars were all half in love with Momma.

Johnny made us stuffed Rock Cornish hen for dinner. The only thing is, Rock Cornish hens are these tiny little chickens, and you have to buy one for each person, and Johnny found out it would cost a fortune and even then there'd be barely a scrap left over for Fenway. So he bought one giant hen of a turkey and called it stuffed Rock Cornish turkey broad.

After dinner, since truck-stop traffic is slow on Saturday nights, we all played poker for M & M's.

Tag, of course, was a cardsharp. He shuffled like dealers in the movies, with fancy bridges and all, and he dealt one-handed, and he had a perfect poker face.

On the last hand, Tag dealt a five-card draw in about nine seconds flat. Deuces were wild. We were all holding our cards tight and low — family or no family, nobody trusted anybody. Stephanie was squirming in her seat; she'd probably drawn an ace, and we all had to know there was something earth-shattering in her hand.

Johnny's face was absolutely grim, so you didn't know if he was covering up a winning hand or if his ulcer was just kicking up. Momma's free hand was under the table, and she was counting on her fingers. Then Johnny placed a bet — he must have something there besides an ulcer. Dad raised him one yellow (yellow and oranges were worth two browns). Somebody had to nudge Momma when it was her turn, and she kicked in two greens, which meant that either she had a dynamite hand, or she'd forgotten that greens were lots more expensive than the other colors.

Tag's face was as blank as a Cabbage Patch Doll's, and he saw Momma's two greens and raised two more. Stephanie stayed in, Dad folded, I folded, Momma dropped two cards face up and was thrown out of the hand, and then it was just Stephanie, Johnny, and Tag.

When I tell you Stephanie was out of her league, I mean it kindly. Would I ever say anything mean about my favorite cousin? But she was betting piles of M & M's, and when I leaned into her hand I saw she had an ace, a king, a queen, a six, and a four, in about eighteen different suits. She probably thought she had some kind of royal straight going. I told her she should just flush the whole thing down the toilet, and for once she listened to me.

That left Johnny and Tag. There was a delicious pile of M & M's in the center of the table. Momma and Dad were holding hands and feeding each other browns — from her pile, not his, of course.

Then Tag said, "Johnny, are you conning me?"

"Could be." Johnny peered over the top of the half-glasses he used just for seeing things up close, but his eyes didn't give away a clue. The moment of truth. I had to crane my neck to see Tag's cards. He was holding three tens and a pair of sixes, but what did Johnny have? Tag saw Johnny's bet, twenty M & M's of all colors, and he raised him five.

Aha! That fired Johnny up, and he slid his whole stake into the center of the table. The tension was so thick you could chisel it off in chunks. COCA-COLA flashed on and off in neon, and Tag had to make a decision, quick.

The little old fox, the tycoon, sized up the competition — and folded. Johnny laid down his hand: a pair of eights! He raked in the whole rainbow mountain of candy with this greedy gurgle of a sound from deep in his throat, while Tag grew smaller and smaller before our eyes.

But on Monday Tag was out at his roadside stand, selling plastic sandwich bags stuffed full of M & M's. Propped up on a table was a fresh new sign: TAKE SOME CANDY TO THOSE SWEET BABIES AT HOME FOR ONLY HALF A BUCK A BAG.

ELEVEN

The restaurant was empty except for Pawnee, who sat in a booth reading the Sunday paper and nursing a glass of iced tea. It was almost two o'clock on a slow, slow day.

"Hey, Tag, put down the funnies a minute. I want to talk to you," I insisted.

"What?" He rustled the paper.

"Listen, since you don't work on Sundays, there's no reason why you can't come with me somewhere."

"Where?" he asked, suspiciously. His head was still buried in the funnies, but I could tell he was interested.

"To the train depot."

He slammed the paper down on the counter. "Now what do I want to go to the train depot for?"

Well, there was no real way to explain, other than to say that this was my favorite spot in Spinner, and it was no use taking Stephanie, and there was this conductor who was a perfect example of someone transplanted from half a century ago to the tail end of the twentieth, and he was just someone Tag ought to meet. But did I tell Tag all this? Oh no. I just said, "Because I said so, that's why."

Those were fighting words for Taggert Layton. He crossed his arms over his chest, those skinny little chicken-bone arms with the big biceps that pop out of nowhere like goiters, and I could see that it would take a forklift to move him down to the depot.

"Personally, I don't care if you go or not. I'm going anyway. And then I'm going over to the Wall-Mart discount store across from the depot, where you can buy things cheap — combs, Life Savers, gum, notepads, pencils, lots of stuff. I need a few supplies," I said, looking off into the wild blue.

"Cheap?"

"Dirt cheap. And there might be a flea market on Sunday over near the depot. You never know what might turn up at a flea market. Dirt cheap."

Tag went into the kitchen and fixed himself three pieces of toast, one with grape jelly, one with strawberry, and one with honey. He carefully recorded the price on his tab, which we had taped to the cash register.

Pawnee folded his paper and came up to the register with a couple of limp dollar bills he'd pulled out of the band of his cowboy hat. "Gimme a pack of Marlboros," he said, helping himself to some free matches. He pulled the cellophane string at the top of the pack, slipped the matches into the cigarette wrapper, and rolled the whole thing deftly into the sleeve of his T-shirt. "Guess I'll see you kids next week. I'll be coming through here about Wednesday. Johnny fixing meatloaf on Wednesday?"

"It's a tradition," I promised.

"Well, save me a good hunk, an end piece. So, kid," he said, turning to Tag, "it's a real bunk day, huh? Whatcha gonna do? You fixin' to go down to that train depot place?"

"I guess so," Tag said glumly.

"Well, clang that bell once for old Pawnee, hear?" He waved to us from the door, and again from the cab of his truck as he started down the lonesome Sunday road.

Mr. Malroy, despite the 102° temperature, was decked out in his navy blue conductor's uniform. It was frayed at the cuffs and shiny at the seat, and it must have fit him better around the middle years ago, but still it looked just right on him. One glance at Mr. Malroy and I understood how Momma felt about uniforms. Even the limp gold braid at his shoulders was impressive, and his black wing-tip shoes were shined to a high polish.

He smiled when he saw us coming. Johnny dropped us off and headed for the Pizza Hut, which was the only restaurant he trusted in Spinner. Probably because the national headquarters of Pizza Hut are in Wichita.

"Good afternoon, miss, mister," the conductor said. "Are you coming aboard?"

"Is he kidding?" Tag whispered.

"Absolutely not," I snapped, shoving Tag ahead of me. He started up the first step.

"Ho, wait a minute, son," said Mr. Malroy. "You got to have a ticket."

Tag shot me a nasty look, but Mr. Malroy reached into his pocket and pulled out two well-worn tickets.

"Here you go. The conductor inside will collect the tickets after the trip gets under way."

We climbed the steep steps into the passenger car. I knew Mr. Malroy would let us explore the locomotive later, but we had to do things in their proper order on his railroad. Outside, we saw him pacing back and forth, yelling, *"All a-boar-rd!"*

Tag loved the car right away. He ran his hands over

108

the smooth red velvet seats and sank into one that had been worn in by bodies much larger than his. His feet touched the brown leather footrest only if he slouched way down.

There was a deep quiet in the coach; even our heartbeats were muffled by the immense velvet seats, the flocked wallpaper, and the thick red carpet. I slid out of my sandals to squirm my feet around in that soft wool.

Tag climbed over me and, like a kid, had to touch everything. I let it go until he ran his hand the whole length of a brass rail at the back of the coach. "For Pete's sake, Tag, keep your grubby hands to yourself. Can't you see how Mr. Malroy has polished that thing up like glass?"

Once more we heard, "*All a-boar-rd!*" but apparently we were to be the only passengers. We felt two stout raps on the flank of the car, Mr. Malroy's signal to the engineer that everyone was aboard. He hoisted himself up the steps with surprising ease, considering that he had to be close to eighty. We watched him slide the door open to the locomotive.

"He's talking to the engineer now," I whispered. Somehow the deep silence of the velvet required soft voices. "He's telling him all's clear for departure."

"What engineer?" Tag asked, craning his neck. "There's nobody up there."

"Haven't you got even a shred of imagination?"

Everything was apparently okay with the engineer, so Mr. Malroy closed that door and slid open the one to our coach. "Afternoon, folks," he said amiably. "First stop, Elgar, then Brooksville, El Dorado, Andover, Wellington, last stop Ponca City. Where to, miss?"

"Wellington."

"You, son?"

"Uh, Ponca City." Tag looked at me smugly.

"Bad news at Ponca City. We got some switching trouble, but I believe we'll get it patched up before the train's due to pull in." He drew a gold watch with a chain out of his breast pocket. "Plenty of time," he assured us, stuffing the watch back. "*Tickets!*"

We handed over our tickets. Mr. Malroy continued down the aisle, stopping at each seat on the coach. Finally he came back and perched on the armrest of the seat across from us.

"Did you ever think where Kansas would be without the railroad?" he said.

"In Missouri?" Tag suggested.

"In Missouri!" Mr. Malroy shook with laughter, and the shiny buttons around his middle strained sorely. His laughter stopped as suddenly as it began. "There's nothing more important to the economy of this great nation than the railroad."

Tag said, "My dad's a truck driver."

"Oh, is he now? Well, how do you think they get the goods to the trucks? Every one of those grand manufacturers and the big farm co-ops and your major grain elevators, they all back up to railroad tracks. We move the lifeblood of this nation down thousands of miles of track, and the trucks pick up the goods for the short hauls where there aren't any tracks. Believe it."

Tag didn't look like he believed it.

"Oh, but the days of the grand passenger trains are gone," Mr. Malroy said, pulling a huge rumpled red handkerchief from his back pocket. He dabbed at his eyes and blew his nose soundly. "Gone. Why, I remember when President Woodrow Wilson came through here in the prettiest coach you ever saw. Painted yellow, it was, and all the upholstery was white. And the world-renowned actress, Sarah Bernhardt, she had an aunt over in Elgar, and she came through whenever she could, with a whole car full of luggage and packages for the folks in Elgar."

Tag asked, "Did you ever have any baseball players on your train?"

"Did we! Why, it was maybe 1940, '41 when the great Ted Williams rode in this car."

"Ted Williams? No kidding? Ted Williams of the Red Sox? He rode *this* car?"

"As I recollect, he sat in that very seat. Yours, or the one behind you, sure enough."

"Wow!" Tag cried. "This is unbelievable. Wait till I tell my dad!"

"Say, son, isn't that a Red Sox cap you're wearing?" Mr. Malroy asked.

"Yes, sir," said Tag, beaming.

"Can you beat that coincidence?" Mr. Malroy said, chuckling. "Well, the railroad's full of romance, son, it's full of romance."

TWELVE

I was in charge of local arrangements for the Beach Boys' concert tour. They liked thick rare steaks served backstage right after each performance. Johnny had his hibachi set up behind the scrim. Smoke curled up into the lights of the show. Just as Johnny was lifting his machete to attack the side of beef and tame it into T-bones, I woke up: there was something out there.

I bolted up in my bed, my ears alert as a hound dog's. Footsteps. Heavy footsteps trying to be light, trying not to grind the gravel of our lot, trying not to upset a single stone. I pulled back a corner of the curtain. A large man had just passed my window, tiptoeing like a clumsy Frankenstein. He was heading — where? — for another cottage? Maybe he was a hobo needing a place to sleep for the night. But something said no. Even in the dark, with just a memory of light from the sliver of a moon, which was so high up in the sky that it was almost ready to give way to morning — even in that light I sensed that the man wasn't a bum. There was nothing untied about him, no clothes flapping or trailing behind him. He wore something all one piece — overalls, and high-top tennis shoes. He walked past Green Cottage 5 and stopped in front of the next cottage. He seemed to be looking it over carefully. Then he raised his beefy hand and knocked on the window of Red Cottage 4. Cee Dubyah!

I pulled on my jeans and a loose T-shirt and stole past Stephanie. The night was almost cool, like it was forgiving the stones under my feet for being lumps of coal during the day. Crickets sang their summer song, stopping for only a second as I passed their love nests. By now Cee Dubyah was inside Tag's cottage. The door was wide open, and barely outlined in the darkness was the giant Cee Dubyah with Tag scooped up in his arms like a puppy. Fenway circled them both.

I tried to look away but couldn't. I was drawn back to those two — Tag with his legs wrapped around his father's waist, and their faces as close to each other as a bow to a violin.

But they never noticed me out there in the dark, and soon they fell to whispering and talking in low mahogany tones, and I had to strain to catch as much as possible.

"You come for me, Cee Dubyah? I can be ready in thirty seconds."

"Not yet, son. Just wanted to see how you're getting along."

"Aw, I'm doing okay. I made a clean profit, more than fifty dollars already after I pay them for my meals."

"Are they giving you any hassles, son?"

"The one, Dovi, she's real bossy. She thinks she's in charge of the world. But I figured out how to get her to do my laundry every Sunday."

He figured out!

"And she warned me when the cops came looking for me with a picture."

"Yeah, well, that's what I got to talk to you about." Cee Dubyah put Tag down and closed the door. I had to move to the window where it was open around the air conditioner Tag never bothered to turn on, and hook my ear to the opening. Cee Dubyah talked up louder anyway, since the door was closed.

"Your mother, she's missing you, son. Bonnie too."

Bonnie?

"Look, Tag, my boy. I know I did the right thing taking you away, because your mother wouldn't of let me have you. But you see what's happening here?"

"What, Cee Dubyah?"

"Well, they're acting like I'm some kind of criminal, sending the police out for me and all. I'm gonna get caught. I can't disappear forever and never get back to driving my truck, and when they find me, do you think a judge is gonna let you come live with a man who's a kidnapper?"

"It's not kidnapping when it's your own kid," Tag said.

"I know that and you know that, but your mother doesn't, and those cops don't, and a judge sure won't, because —" he paused as if he were looking for just the right way to put what he had to say. "Your mother has the law on her side."

"But nobody ever asked me who I want to live with," Tag cried, and whatever else he said was muffled in his father's chest.

After a while Cee Dubyah said, "Here's what I got to do, son. I'm turning myself in, because I can't keep you holed up here, and I can't keep running, and there's nowhere we can get to that they won't find us."

"We could go to Boston, Massachusetts," Tag said in a tiny voice.

"No, son."

"All right," Tag said, back in command of himself. "What's the plan? We gotta have a plan."

"That's my boy. I'll just catch a few winks here. You think you can find a corner of that bed for me for an hour or two? Then I'll head back to Wichita, and me and the lawyer will go to the police."

"They gonna put you in the slammer, Cee Dubyah?"

"Naw," he said, without much conviction. "Then the lawyer and me are gonna start building an airtight case for you to come live with me. If your mother won't let me have you full-time, well then, we'll work on half-time, or summer-time, or whatever we can wheedle outta her, because she sure knows now that you and I belong together. Now don't you worry, we'll work it out . . . it'll be all right . . . we'll be two peas in a pod again." Cee Dubyah crooned it over and over, like a lullaby, and pretty soon I heard this little crinkling of bedsprings as Cee Dubyah put Tag down, then a ferocious groaning of the springs under Cee Dubyah.

I leaned my back against an oak tree out behind the cottages to wait for the sun, but even so I missed Cee Dubyah's leaving. I hoped Tag had, too.

Tag never said a word about his middle-of-the-night visitor, but I had to tell Stephanie and Momma that the ax was about to fall. I went the long way around from the walk-in freezer to Tag's shop that morning. There he was squeezing one of Johnny's lemons into a can of Coke and telling some trucker that this was the refreshing new taste sensation from Fort Lauderdale, Florida. He licked the lemon juice off his grubby fingers and puckered his whole face up.

"Real sanitary conditions here," the trucker said, giving way to a big yawn.

"You look a little sleepy, sir," Tag told the driver. "That's the curse of being on the road." Again, it sounded just like Cee Dubyah talking.

"I could use a package of No-Doz," the driver conceded.

"Hey, forget No-Doz." Tag fished around in his carton and pulled out a package of Bubble Yum. "Try this. I reckon nobody can fall asleep while he's chewing and blowing bubbles."

I smiled to myself as the man gave Tag a quarter for the gum and headed back to his truck with the refreshing new taste sensation sloshing around in the can.

"Hold it!" Tag said. He wrote something on a slip of paper.

"What's this?" the trucker asked, stretching to get the kinks out of his long, lean body.

"It's a receipt."

"For twenty-five cents' worth of gum?"

"Sure. It's a tax-deductible business expense," Tag assured him. "Just a little service I give my best customers." The trucker stuffed the receipt in his shirt pocket, behind his cigarettes, and chuckled all the way back to his cab. I could just picture him blowing purple bubbles from Spinner to Oklahoma City.

Back in the Pig-Out, I couldn't delay it any longer. I had to tell Momma about Cee Dubyah.

"Oh, that poor sweet child," she said, while Stephanie gasped and added something to her fiction novel. "Did Cee Dubyah say anything about somebody coming for Tag, or are we to have him until Tag gets married?"

I hadn't given it a thought, but it's true that Cee Dubyah never did tell Tag exactly what was going to happen to him.

"He'll come for Tag," Stephanie said.

"How can he, if he's in custody?" asked Momma.

We talked about it off and on while we got ready for the lunch crowd, and before the first onslaught I took Tag's lunch out to him. We'd started doing that so Tag wouldn't miss any of the business he stole away from us. Stephanie and I packed him up a couple of pieces of fried chicken — Johnny had become a master of fried chicken that was light and crisp on the outside, but you had to eat it carefully because you might bite into a grease pocket that would spurt hot stuff into somebody else's hair. Along with the chicken we brought him a cup of cole slaw, a nectarine, and a piece of pecan pie. Momma said this was the $1.50 Blue Plate Special, which cost everyone else $4.25.

"Chicken again?" Tag said, wrinkling up his nose. "I was hoping for a peanut butter and jelly."

I almost yelled, "You're the most ungrateful child!" But then I flashed on Tag curled around Cee Dubyah's waist, and I bit my lip to hold back the words. Instead I said, "What have you conned Johnny out of this morning?" I noticed Tag had added a line of potato chips and Fritos in little twenty-five-cent bags. I remembered Johnny asking me to order these, but come to think of it, we'd never sold them in the Pig-Out.

"I buy them from Johnny at cost," Tag said simply. Fenway stood on his hind legs, lapping water from the ice bucket, raising his leg to let it go, then lapping more water, like a perfectly efficient waterworks system.

"Gross, Fenway!" I said.

"Aw, leave him alone."

Trucks were pulling up behind the restaurant, and

120

soon Stephanie leaned out the door and signaled for me to get to work. The Pig-Out was jumping with truckers anxious to get back on the road and collect for their long hauls.

The hours flew by — noon, one o'clock, two — until finally the place cleared out and we could start mopping up for dinner.

Just then Tag came to the door carrying Fenway, like a hunter with a deer draped across his arms, only Tag's face was chalk white, and his eyes were huge and sunken.

"A car hit him," Tag said.

"Momma, come quick! Fenway got run over!" The dog hung limply, overflowing Tag's arms. Momma felt for a pulse and shook her head.

"Oh — my — Lord!" Stephanie cried. Tag just stood there like a statue.

Johnny came out front and quickly sized up the situation. Without a word he lifted Fenway from Tag's arms and took the pup out back somewhere. Momma pulled Tag to her and stroked his head, not saying much.

Tag didn't make a sound either, just shook a little, and when Momma shifted him around the top of her apron was soaked gray. "Maybe it's time for you to go home," Momma said softly.

121

Something was sizzling on the grill and Stephanie went to the kitchen, leaving the doors to swing back and forth with a lonesome swoosh.

With Johnny out back taking care of Fenway and Stephanie busy in the kitchen and Momma holding Tag, I'd never felt more useless in my life.

THIRTEEN

wwwwwwwwwwwwwwwwwwwwwwwwwwwwwwwwwwwwwwww

I knew who she was as soon as she walked in that night, wearing a crisp yellow jump suit and a raspberry-and-lemon-sherbet shirt rolled up at the cuffs. The freckles gave her away. She had long plum nails, and her right pinkie was gold-speckled. Her hair was feathered back and layered to her shoulders. I was pretty sure she wasn't a natural blonde. She warmed the air around her with delicate driver-sweat and some perfume that smelled like baby powder.

There was this little round girl with her, about five, wearing a snug halter top and shorts and carrying a stuffed Snoopy with sunglasses.

The one lone truck driver left after dinner looked the woman over good and hard, until his eyes fell on the little dumpling of a girl and then trailed back to his newspaper.

"Who's in charge here?" the woman asked. She had a voice deeper than I'd expected for such pastel fluff clothes.

Momma stood up.

"You?" the woman said. Maybe she'd been expecting a big farm hand kind of woman. "I'm Rosie McFee," she said finally. "Taggert's mother."

"Mommy," the little girl said, "is this where Tag's living, in a restrawnt?" It was Tag's voice all over again — a growl, almost.

"Quiet, baby, hmm?" She turned back to Momma. "You're the owner?"

Momma nodded. "Marilyn Chandler," she said, putting out her hand, which just hung there because the woman was shaking her head back and forth and saying, "My God, Cee Dubyah didn't even know your name. Where is he, Mrs. Chandler? Where's my son?"

"Dovi, go get him," Momma said.

I flew out the back door, tripping over Stephanie and Eddie, who were plastered together on a lawn chair near the walk-in.

First I knocked on Johnny's door. "She's here for him," I whispered. My heart was thumping like an Indian war drum as I reached Tag's cottage. There wasn't a light shining anywhere. I knocked softly, and thought I heard him say come in. He lay in his jeans in the center of the bed, barely taking up any space at all, and with his arms folded under his neck. The room smelled of Fenway and felt heavy with emptiness, like a load you could carry on your back.

"Your momma's here, Tag. Bonnie too." He turned over onto his stomach. "She seems very nice. She's so pretty." Tag sat up, reached under his pillow for his Red Sox shirt, and slipped it over his head. It fell around him like a tent — not like a shirt at all, just a rag that didn't remember anybody's shape. He stood up and turned away to tuck the shirt in. Even tucked in, it seemed sad the way the top gaped open over his scrawny neck. I thought maybe it was Cee Dubyah's shirt. The little gold cross lay flat on the ribbing.

He picked up a backpack stuffed with clothes and probably all the merchandise from his shop that he could ram into it. There was also a shopping bag, which I grabbed before he could start his macho act and try to carry it all.

"Whatever's left belongs to you anyway," he said. He slapped his leg once — to call Fenway? — then remembered.

We trooped over to the restaurant. Anybody driving by would have thought we were a couple of scouts heading for a camp-out in the woods.

From the kitchen we heard murmurs of mothertalk,

an easy give-and-take, which made me feel a little better about this McFee woman whose house Tag would be sleeping in later that night.

Johnny came in behind us and put his arm around Tag. "What the hey are you doing in here this hour of the night?" he teased Tag.

"I gotta get up early to get ahead of you," Tag shot back as Johnny pushed something — I couldn't see what — into his pocket.

Bonnie spotted his face first, above the swinging door. "Mommy, look!" Tag pushed his way into the dining room. Bonnie ran toward him, stopping shyly just short of his feet. Mrs. McFee encircled them both with her sherbet arms.

"We're going home, Taggert," she said. No scolding, no questions, no hysterics. Just "We're going home."

"And you know what? Mommy says we can stop in El Dorado for a ice cream. And you know what else? She says I can stay up till midnight if I want, and I'm not supposed to be a pest. Isn't that what you said, Mommy? I'm not supposed to be a pest till tomorrow, so you won't want to leave again."

It's funny. I expected some sign from Tag that he hated his mother, or was afraid of her, or some sign from her that she was hateful or scary, but it simply wasn't like that. He let her kiss his forehead, as embarrassed as most kids are when their parents slobber over them, and then he said proudly, "Guess what. I've been selling stuff again. I've got over fifty dollars."

"Ooooh, Taggert, one day you're going to be a rich, rich man," his mother beamed. "Will you buy us a house by the ocean? How about Malibu Beach, over in California?"

Tag shook his head. "Boston, Massachusetts," he said, and I was proud of his mother for not asking why Boston. Or maybe she already knew about Tag and Cee Dubyah's plans at Fenway Park.

Now Mrs. McFee shook Momma's hand and said, "Thank you for looking after Taggert."

"He doesn't need looking after. He takes good care of himself," Momma said, smiling toward Tag.

"Well." Mrs. McFee held her children tightly by the hand. It was as if she'd never be able to let either of them out of her sight again. And they were gone.

The next day dragged by. More than once I found myself looking for Tag out by the road, or trying to see what was missing that he might be selling out from under us. At lunchtime I automatically started fixing a plate for him, and when Stephanie asked what I was doing I said something like, "What is it, a big sin if I want to have a decent lunch for a change, instead of a bite of this and a bite of that?" But Stephanie knew, I think.

We had a pretty steady dinner bunch in and out. Some customers were even stopping at the Pig-Out instead of the Star Cafe twenty miles up the highway, because it was Wednesday, meatloaf day, and Johnny's meatloaf was becoming a legend in its own time. I had to remember to save an end piece for Pawnee.

Momma and Johnny were in the kitchen putting up salads, and Johnny was swearing at the lettuce — which, the best we could tell out in the diner, seemed to have rusty brown spots all the way through it. "Holy shee, what did the farmer do, grow this stuff at the county dump? Hogs would turn up their snouts at it."

"Shh, Johnny," we heard Momma whisper, while the customers all had a good chuckle and said no, thank you to the salads that came with the meatloaf.

Emile Joe Hunter said his stomach was a little squeamish. He couldn't face anything with gravy, so he'd just have a bacon, lettuce, and tomato sandwich. "But, uh," Emile Joe said, "you know."

I shouted through the pass-through, "BLT, burn the bacon, heavy on the mayo, fry the tomato, and hold the lettuce."

"You need a God-blessed computer back here when you feed me orders like that," Johnny muttered, and I heard the cold bacon slap the grill, then the forgiving sizzle.

Palmer came in just then looking for Tag. "Where is that kid? He's always over at my station by six to mop up."

"He's gone home," I said, flying by with a couple of burgers crowding each other off a plate. "Want something to eat, Palm?"

"I don't want anything to eat. I want my clean-up boy."

Stephanie had just picked up a plate with a dense hunk of meatloaf dominating a little hill of mashed potatoes and a few scrawny gray-green beans. She waved the steam away from Palmer's face. "You see," she began explaining like a teacher with a class full of students who aren't too quick, "Tag is a victim of contemporary divorce statistics. It's a question of maternal or paternal custody."

Palmer looked from Stephanie to me. "What's she talking about?" He tore into a package of saltines on the counter and stuffed a whole cracker into his mouth.

"Is that my dinner?" some guy at the end of the counter asked. The steam had died off by the time Stephanie got it to him. "I love cold meatloaf," the trucker said. "Sits there in my gut like somebody poured me full of lead."

"What she means, Palmer, is that Tag wants to live with his father, but the law's got him living with his mother, so that's where he is now."

"Well, why didn't she say that?" Palmer asked.

I gave him a glass of ice water to wash down the cracker crumbs hanging from his mouth. "Because she's a city girl, Palm. In the city things look much more complicated."

"Oh, good grief," Stephanie snorted, "Wichita isn't exactly New York City, you know."

"It's not even Philly," one of the customers said. "Or New Orleans," which he pronounced "Nawlins."

"But it *is* Oklahoma City," one of the other guys, Jenkins, said. "Same town, in two different states."

"Am I thickheaded today?" asked Palmer. "Nobody's making any sense. Hand me a toothpick, would you, Dovi?"

"Anything else we can get you for free?" I retorted. "Want to use the phone?"

"Now why would I do that when I've got my own phone just across the road? Well, I'd better get over there since there's nobody else to mop up."

"Aren't you having your usual bowl of chili?" asked

130

Stephanie. "Johnny made it fresh just last Monday." She'd learned to hold three glasses in the flat of her hand, and now she was filling them with ice, dropping only every other piece on the floor.

"I don't need no chili today. The wife's visiting her sister up in Iowa, so I'm going to a real restaurant for dinner. Well, see you girls tomorrow."

Scurrying around the diner, we caught a glimpse of him dashing between cars to the Gas Fast across the highway. Stephanie turned to the audience at large. "Gentlemen, wouldn't you agree that that was, without a doubt, *the* rudest thing in the world? Imagine him sitting here" — she twirled around, hands extended, to take in the entire piggish kingdom — "and telling us he's going to be dining at a *real* restaurant tonight. What does he think you guys are doing here?"

"We're eating, but we ain't dining," Emile Joe said.

I posed the corker: "Let's face it, Steph. If you had your choice of all the restaurants in the world, would you pick the Pig-Out Inn?"

"Well, *I*, of course, would pick Maxim's, in Gay Paree." She slid a pickle wafer off someone's cheeseburger platter and sucked on it dreamily. "I guess my second choice would be Steak and Ale, where these gorgeous hunks bring you a menu engraved on a meat cleaver — can you believe it, a meat cleaver! I mean, this is a classy place on a four-lane divided road running right through Wichita."

"Steak and Ale? They got the same thing in Oklahoma City," Jenkins said. From the juke box, Willie and Julio crooned, "For all the girls we've loved before . . ."

Two days later a letter came from Hopkins, Corrwall, Punchess & Bailey, Attorneys-at-Law, saying that Momma was to appear in Wichita, in Family Court, to give a deposition on Tag.

FOURTEEN

~~~~~~

Momma gave Johnny last-minute instructions before we left. "You're not to close up before eight o'clock at night, and hang on to all the receipts and bills for Mike, and don't experiment with any new recipes until I get back and can explain them away. Oh, and don't forget to call McCrary about the frozen fries. And be sure not to let Stephanie go off this property with that young soldier."

"Oh, Aunt Marilyn."

Momma flew around the diner, wiping here, tucking there, and helping herself to a handful of ten-dollar bills from the till. She wore what she called her Saturday matinée clothes — a white linen suit with a silky turquoise blouse that wasn't exactly low, but showed more of Momma than Dad approved of, and dressy white sandals with low heels. She had a rope of heavy turquoise and beige and white beads around her neck — the kind that looked elegant on her, but would have been like an anchor on me, yanking me down and underwater.

"Oh, and Johnny," she warned, spit-curling a trail of hair escaping from her chignon, "don't cuss at the customers. Stephanie, see that he doesn't cuss."

"Oh, I will," Stephanie promised. She'd have made a terrific warden.

"And Johnny, when that boyfriend of Stephanie's comes by as soon as I'm out of sight, you see that they keep all four feet squarely on the ground."

"Aunt Marilyn!" Stephanie looked shocked, and I had to get out of there before I fell apart laughing.

Momma doesn't believe in speed limits — but then, along with her theories on the sun and the moon, she doesn't understand radar either. So if there's no cop in sight she assumes she's free to drive eighty miles per hour, unless it means climbing up the back of some truck ahead of us.

We had the windows rolled down, and at eighty the hot wind was whipping through the car and half our words flew out the window, but I distinctly heard Momma say, "What do you think, Dovi? Is the restaurant business working out for us?"

"Well, are we making a profit yet?" I shouted.

"We can make expenses, meet our mortgage, pay Johnny, but—"

"We're not getting rich."

"No. It wouldn't really be any fun if we were."

"You'd give it all away anyway, Momma."

"I suppose I would. Things are no better for the migrant workers in western Kansas than they were in Oklahoma during the *Grapes of Wrath* days, you know."

Well, I had to nip that one quickly, because the way Momma's mind was spinning, we'd be out of the Pig-Out and into a grocery store in Medicine Lodge, Kansas, before the first winter freeze. "We never rent the cottages, of course, but I think the diner does really well for us, Momma. Look, without it Johnny would be collecting unemployment. Face it, who else would hire a crab like him? And where would Tag have been without our place?"

We both fell silent thinking about Tag and what lay ahead for him and for Momma in court later that day.

The deposition was given in Judge Edgar Bohanan's office — his chambers, they called it. Cee Dubyah's lawyer was there, and Mrs. McFee's lawyer, and someone taking it all down on a machine.

"Good afternoon, Your Honor," Momma said, extending her hand across the judge's desk. She looked and sounded very self-assured and worldly, not at all like a person who had no idea what radar was. "This is my daughter, Dovi Chandler."

The judge, who was wearing a business suit instead of one of those graduation gowns, nodded, then excused me curtly.

"Your Honor, I would prefer to have my daughter remain, since her contact with the young man in question was far more extensive than my own."

"Very well," Judge Bohanan sighed. "Court reporter, note for the record that the deposition was given jointly by the two ladies. State your full names, please."

And on it went. We were asked the most incredibly exact and boring details about Tag: day, hour, and minute of his arrival; how he looked; how he was dressed. Were there any visible marks on him? Was his hair full and healthy-looking, or patchy? Was his skin clear and clean, or mottled and pocked? Were there any signs of malnourishment? Did his shoes seem too tight?

My guess was that Cee Dubyah's lawyer was trying to build a case against Mrs. McFee's mothering, but we couldn't help out there much, because Tag came to us looking like a regular nine-year-old kid—scruffy, but not pitiful; hardly some boy out of the pages of *Oliver Twist*.

Then we were asked to describe, to the best of our knowledge, Tag's relationship with his father, and I found myself swallowing back tears as I told these legal hounds, who were as hungry for information as our truckers were for meatloaf, about what I saw and heard eavesdropping outside Tag's cottage.

Next they wanted to know, in tiny bites of detail, everything about Tag's daily schedule at our place. I couldn't lie — I was under oath — but I also couldn't tell them about some of his cons and flim-flam dealings, or the beer.

"He's a very enterprising boy," Momma said, "quite self-sufficient. He saw that he had some time to fill, so he set up a roadside business."

"Doing what?" Judge Bohanan asked.

I jumped in. "Selling gum. He said it was better than No-Doz to keep the truckers awake." Those serious faces cracked a bit for quick smiles. "And he sold cold drinks."

"Like?"

"Like Coca-Cola, Dr. Pepper. He bought them at cost and sold them cheaper than we could in the restaurant," Momma explained.

"And," I added, "he had a deal with the gas station across the road to mop the place in trade for ice to keep the Cokes cold."

"He's a clever child," said Momma.

"Enterprising says it well," the judge responded, dryly.

"He's so enterprising, Your Honor, that he figured out a way to get me to wash his clothes for him." Well, that wasn't actually a lie, because Tag truly believed he'd conned me into doing his laundry, even if I knew better.

It went on like this, with us answering their questions honestly, but also not quite telling them everything. Then they wanted to know what it was like when Tag's mother came for him. Was he happy to see her, or sad? Did he resist going with her? Did they seem to have a decent attitude toward each other? Did they seem comfortable together? Did she threaten or force or intimidate him in any way? Did he seem loving and respectful, or did he seem frightened, nervous, or angry?

This part was hard, because I couldn't honestly say anything against Mrs. McFee, except that I thought her gold nail was gross. The thing is, she seemed better than the average mother, and Tag seemed to like her just fine.

But liking your mother just fine, and adoring the father you wanted to be just like — these were two different things.

Then came the clincher. The judge said, "Now, Mrs. Chandler and Miss Chandler, I'm going to ask you a question, and you may refuse to answer if you wish. One at a time, please. In your opinion, would Taggert Layton's needs be better met with his father, or with his mother?"

Momma thought for the longest time, then finally replied, "Both of Tag's parents love him deeply. His father is a kind and decent man. But he is on the road most of the time, and it is my opinion, regretfully, that Tag would be better off with his mother and sister in a steady, dependable home."

Momma, the nomad, said this? I couldn't believe it!

"Miss Chandler?"

I was sure this was the hardest thing I'd ever been asked to do. "Your Honor, sir, if you've ever seen Tag and Cee Dubyah together, then you know what it means when someone says, 'They're like two peas in a pod.'" I didn't think Cee Dubyah would mind if I borrowed his words. "Tag told me there were days when they spent nine, ten, eleven hours in the truck, barely talking. But he never got bored to death, because there's this easy silence between Tag and his father. They could be comparing trees along the road, or counting oil pumps, or commenting on some weird road sign, all without having to say a word."

Judge Bohanan leaned way forward in his seat, hanging on every word. Everyone was, except for Mrs. McFee's lawyer, who was flicking something out from under his nails.

I shifted around, wondering how to say the rest. "Tag would be okay with his mother. She seems like a nice lady, and I like the way she didn't yell at him when she came to get him, or ask him a thousand questions, especially the big one about why he left her to go with his father." I paused, held my finger up to signal that I wasn't done, and I thought a minute about Tag wrapped around Cee Dubyah's waist, and the sweet creaking bedsprings, and that wilted stamp-sized note that Tag had hidden in the air conditioner, and that I now fingered in the pocket of my skirt. And I knew I couldn't say it any plainer. "Sir, Cee Dubyah and Tag belong together."

"Thank you very much, ladies. You've been most helpful," said Judge Bohanan. The court reporter was hurrying us out of the chambers, flexing her tired fingers, and already the two lawyers had formed a huddle around the judge's desk.

Sitting on a bench outside the courtroom was this massive person in a brown business suit — Cee Dubyah, as I'd never seen him before.

"Cee Dubyah!" Momma cried. "I wouldn't have recognized you. Why, you look so handsome and proper!"

Cee Dubyah came to his feet on gleaming cowboy boots. He grinned at us, but seemed very jittery. "This is the day it all hits the fan," he explained. "This makes it or breaks it, as far as Tag and me goes."

"Good luck, Cee Dubyah," I whispered. "I did my best."

"That's all I can ask. Say, I owe you for Tag's room and all." He reached for his wallet, and had to unbutton his suit jacket to get to it.

"No, no," Momma said — for we weren't under oath any longer — "Tag paid every penny from his earnings." She stood on her toes and straightened Cee Dubyah's tie. "Now, you just go in there and make the most of whatever the judge decides."

FIFTEEN

Stephanie took the red stuff off and painted her toe-nails to match her fingernails to match her lipstick to match her shocking-pink pants. Eddie was on his way for their first date Off the Grounds. They were going to the Spinner movie. There was one movie in town, and it changed every Thursday; this was only Friday, so it was still pretty hot stuff. Momma gave them exactly one hour from the close of the movie (11:14) to the opening of the door of the Pig-Out, where she'd be waiting like Mother Superior at the gates of the convent.

I fumbled through the desk drawer for my sunglasses. "Your toenails are blinding me," I explained. "I hope Eddie's farsighted."

"Eddie, for your information, has perfect vision."

I stared at her, trying not to smile. It's pretty hard to take anyone seriously when she's got wads of cotton stuffed between her toes, making her feet look about nineteen inches wide.

"By the way, Stephanie, I forgot to tell you something about my trip to Wichita." I hadn't really forgotten. I was just saving it up for a terrible moment like this. "Guess what I did."

"You went to Steak and Ale?"

"No, it's about a well-known person I talked to on the phone."

"How well known? World famous?" Now she was just a little bit interested.

"Not quite world famous."

Stephanie screwed the nail polish shut and dangled her fingers like wet laundry. "Known throughout the entire state of Kansas?" she guessed.

"No way."

"A famous Wichita athlete? A soccer player, maybe? I know, someone from the Wichita Wings!"

"Not even close."

"You said well known," Stephanie pouted.

"Yeah, but I didn't say who knew him well."

"Aha, it's a 'him'!" she cried. She blew on her nails and pretended now to be bored with the whole subject, so that's when I hit her with it.

"Wayne Firestone."

Stephanie sucked in her breath. "You called Wayne Firestone?"

"Yep."

"Why on God's green earth would you do a thing like that?"

"You made such a big deal about the All Star game. I thought you'd want to know if he won."

"Well, what did he say?"

"You might not like it," I warned.

"Wayne Firestone is a part of the past, Dovi. There is nothing he can say or do that would touch me in any way."

"Okay, but you made me tell you."

Stephanie said, between clenched teeth, "I would strangle you, Cousin Dovi, but my nails are still wet. *Tell!*" Oh, it was going just the way I'd planned.

"Okay." I held an imaginary phone to my ear. "Ring ring. 'May I speak to Wayne? (Pause) Wayne? This is Dovi Chandler.'

" 'Who's Dovi Chandler?' he asked.

" 'Stephanie Fisher's cousin.'

" 'Who's Stephanie Fisher?'

"Well, by now I know I'm talking to a real mental giant, so I said, 'She's about five eight —' "

"Five seven," Stephanie protested.

" '— has long brown hair, brown eyes. She sat behind you in English last year.' "

"Not English. French!" Stephanie cried.

"So he said, 'Oh, you mean Donna Sperling?' "

Stephanie groaned and pulled the cotton out. Her toes snapped back.

" 'Right, I'm Donna Sperling's cousin. Donna wants to know how you did in the All Star game.' Well, all of a sudden I was talking his language, and he jumped into this blow-by-blow.

" 'We did great. Super-fantastic. It was the bottom of the seventh — we only play seven innings, I guess everyone knows that. They were the home team, so we wouldn't get another up-at-bat. There was one out, and they were trailing by a run, and it was now-or-never time, you know what I mean? So, there's a runner on first. Donna told you I'm a first baseman, I guess, and I'm covering the runner close, because he's leading off and he's gonna steal second in a minute. Then this gorilla comes up to bat. I swear, he musta weighed 220 pounds, more like a tackle than a batter, and I'm figuring, well, he's a power hitter. He's either going to hit one over the fence, and it's all over for us, or he might hit a line drive to right field, and then we've got him, because it would take him about twenty minutes to get his bod' to first. You still listening?'

145

" 'Hanging on every word,' I told Wayne.

" 'So, it happened like a dream. Boink! The bat and ball connect, and it's a line drive just past me into right field. The fielder throws the ball to second — out! — and second throws it to me before Ape Man ever gets there — a double play! I'm telling you, it was a thriller!' "

"Oh mercy, my heart is fluttering with excitement," said Stephanie in a sarcastic monotone. "Honestly, who but a little boy can get so worked up over a silly game?"

"You don't like Wayne Firestone anymore?"

Stephanie sighed patiently. "My dear cousin, I have Eddie Perini now, a member of the United States Army and a licensed radio operator. What on earth would I do with a child like Wayne?"

"I'm really glad you feel that way, Steph, because Wayne said he was going to hang up and call Donna Sperling right away and take her to a show."

The Pig-Out was packed with dinner customers. Some were even travelers who believed that old thing about finding the best food where all the trucks are parked. One of the truckers dropped a quarter into the juke box and brought Glen up to the turntable, and he was gentle on all our minds, calming Momma and me as we raced around the diner trying to keep everyone happy.

Then, with just two stools left at the counter, who should walk in but Cee Dubyah and Tag.

"Taggert Layton!" Momma cried. "Why, I'll bet you've grown two inches since we saw you last!"

Cee Dubyah patted Tag's head proudly. "Had to take him over to Shepler's to buy him some new dungarees."

"Jeans, Cee Dubyah, Levi's," Tag said in that gritty voice I'd missed hearing. "Nobody but you calls 'em dungarees."

"Hoo boy, the kid's getting cheeky," said Cee Dubyah with a grin.

Momma brought them each a bowl of vegetable soup and a mounded basket of crackers. "We want to hear how things are going, but as you can see —"

"Aw, we got plenty of time. Me and Tag will just sit here until everybody clears out."

Well, we rushed the crowd through their dinners, shouting orders to Johnny so fast that he burst through the swinging doors and hollered, "*Hold it!* Y'all sit tight on your rear ends, and nobody order anything until I catch up, hear? I'll let you know when I'm ready. Hi ya, Tag."

The regulars, of course, were used to Johnny, but

the travelers didn't know what to make of him and cowered in their booths like circus tigers under a tamer's whip. We waited for a shout from Johnny that he was ready, and finally he rang a bell. We had expected something a lot more dramatic, but there was this little bell on the pass-through, the kind you see at a Holiday Inn when they're trying to get someone to carry an old lady's suitcases. So we heard this dainty little tinkle, followed by "Kitchen's open again, folks. Lay it on me!"

Momma and I shifted through our order books and let him have it: hot beef san, hold the mashed, give 'im fries. Pair of cheeseburgers riding on one horse, fries, fry 'em extra crisp. Dinner steak, burn it, no salt. Grilled cheese san on rye, got that? *Rye*, hold the pickles and slaw. We were merciless. Well, Johnny was awfully quiet back there, so I peeked in the pass-through to see whether he'd just given up and gone bowling. There was Tag hustling around the kitchen, flipping burgers, buttering bread, fixing plates for Johnny.

Cee Dubyah crouched down to see into the kitchen and watch his son in action. "That boy's somethin' else," he chuckled. "He'll double your output before you know it."

"We've sure missed him," I admitted, grabbing up their empty soup bowls. Tag's was bone-dry, except he'd left all the lima beans and all the carrots, lined up on opposite sides of the bowl like rival football squads. "I'm throwing these away," I told Cee Dubyah, "before Tag finds a way to sell them."

After things had slowed down a little, Palmer stopped in for a quick bowl of chili. He wasn't a bit happy to see Tag. "Hey, what happened to you? One day you're my clean-up boy, next day you're gone."

"Sorry, sir," Tag said, trying for the life of him to sound humble. "I had to move on."

"Well, if a guy moves on, he ought to give notice. Two weeks' notice," Palmer grumbled, while the chili steam fogged up his glasses.

Tag said, "I agree with you a hundred and fifty percent, Mr. Palmer, but the circumstances were unavoidable. Tell him, Cee Dubyah."

"Unavoidable," his father agreed.

"So, sir, I'm hoping my moving on so quick won't stand in the way of your writing me a letter of recommendation for when I apply for another job." Tag took a small notebook out of his back pocket and flipped it open like Captain Kirk asking to be beamed up.

Palmer wiped chili down his overalls and took the notebook. "A letter of recommendation? Why sure," he said amicably. Then his eyes narrowed, "If you scoot over there right now and mop the living daylights out of my station."

"Yes, sir!" Tag said. He jumped down from the stool and ran to the door.

"Ever' single corner, ever' nook and cranny," Palmer said. "I want it clean as an Army bunkhouse."

"When I get done, you could eat off the floor, sir." Tag opened the door, then looked back as if it were an afterthought — but I knew he had it planned this way all along. "You don't mind, Mr. Palmer, if my dad fills up at your diesel pump, do you?"

Well, what could Palmer do, with all those truckers in the place hanging on every word, and him looking like a slave driver and a Scrooge, taking advantage of a sweet, innocent nine-year-old kid? "Naw, go ahead, Cee Dubyah. First tank's on the house. But when you come through here next week, all bets are off, hear?"

Everyone finally cleared out, and we turned off the neon sign so no late travelers or bugs would come to our door. We pulled a circle of lawn chairs out in front of the Pig-Out Inn.

Cee Dubyah filled every inch of his chair; if he'd stood up, the chair would have gone with him. And Tag looked like a rag doll thrown into a corner of his chair. His feet barely hit the ground. Johnny took off his shoes and socks — good thing we were outside — and dug his toes into the dry summer earth.

Momma called the meeting to order. "Before Stephanie and that boyfriend of hers come home, we're all eager to hear how things were settled in court."

"Best possible way," Cee Dubyah said.

"You and Tag are together!" I cried, clapping my hands.

"Yes, but that's not the whole picture," Cee Dubyah explained, while Tag fidgeted in his chair. "Here's what that Judge Bohanan said. He said a boy needs a regular, steady home he can come home to after school."

I glared at Momma, who pretended not to see me in the dark.

"A place to bring his friends home to, a place where there's a hot supper ready every day, where he can spread out his homework on a table that he knows is going to be there every night of the week."

"I don't do homework," Tag said.

"But you will, son. Fifth grade isn't any picnic, like fourth grade. Now, that wasn't all the judge said."

"Get to the good part," I urged Cee Dubyah.

"He said it was his opinion —"

"His 'studied opinion,' those were his words," Tag said.

"Whatever. The judge said it sure looked like me and Tag had something good going for us. He said there was this study that said the average American father spends four minutes a week with his kids, and that even though I'm on the road half my life, or more, I always got time for my son. He said I'm sure not the average father."

We all smiled at Cee Dubyah, stuffed in his chair and puffed up with pride.

"What about Bonnie?" I asked.

"Well, honey, Bonnie isn't mine," Cee Dubyah replied. "McFee's her daddy. So," he continued, "Judge Bohanan said the best thing for Tag is a joint custody deal. He'll go with his mother during the school year, and he'll come with me in the summers and other holidays, and weekends we'll work out whatever's best for everybody."

"That sounds like the ideal arrangement, Cee Dubyah," Momma said.

"Well, I disagree." I stood up furiously, overturning my chair. "The judge didn't listen to a word I said."

"Aw, sit down," Johnny commanded. "It looks to me

like you're the one who's not listening. Tell me if I'm wrong, kid. You got the best deal, right?"

Tag squirmed around, but didn't answer Johnny.

"Don't sit there like a pimple on a forehead. Speak up."

"I don't want to," Tag said quietly.

"What's with him?" Johnny asked Cee Dubyah. "All of a sudden the kid with the biggest mouth in Kansas shuts up like a clam."

Cee Dubyah gave Tag a chance to say something, but when he didn't, Cee Dubyah tried to speak for him. "I think what's going on here, Johnny, is that the boy is afraid he's gonna hurt my feelings if he tells his true heart."

I sat down to listen.

"He thinks he's not supposed to want to live with his mother and sister and stepdad. He thinks that a manly guy would want to be on the road all the time, with his real dad." Cee Dubyah paused, gathering up his words. "But deep down, he knows he belongs in one place, at his mother's, during school time, and I reckon he loves his mother. What the kid doesn't know is that, sure, it's okay if he loves his mother, even if I don't."

Tag said, "How come all those hours in the truck, you never said that before?"

"Couldn't trust myself to say it and not drive off the road."

Tag smiled and rearranged himself in the chair, more at home.

"We're going to have fine summers, son, fine, sweet summers."

SIXTEEN

Halfway through the summer the heat set in perma-
nently. You'd wake up on those 90° nights, sweating
just from the sheer effort of sleeping. The wheat was
newly harvested, and all along the highway sunflowers
with big black and yellow faces began sprouting up.
Weeds again. But these were weeds that were pro-
grammed to show up every year, same time, same
place. Emile Joe told me you could snap off a blossom
one year, and if you remembered just which stalk it
came from, the next year you'd find a wound at the
very spot you'd plucked the flower from. Sunflowers
were regular, dependable flowers. They were growing
here long before I ever made my small splash in Spinner, and they'd still be here long after I was gone.

The sunflowers meant it was time to go into town
and register at the high school, just like Tag was prob-

ably doing at his school in Wichita. Momma drove me in, though all the other kids came without parents. A whole pickup full pulled up just ahead of us and unloaded fourteen guys and girls, all dressed alike in shorts and floppy shirts. I, of course, had forced my sweaty body into a gingham skirt and a pink roll-up sleeve blouse, and I looked ridiculous beside the others. The Fourteen stared at me, but no one said hello. They poured into the school and disappeared down the dark hall.

Momma and I stood outside, cupping our hands at our foreheads to block the sun, and looked the building over thoroughly. It was two stories, with air-conditioning boxes outside each small, dark window. The building was made of limestone slabs in a forbidding grayish brown shade. There were water stains etched into the limestone beneath each air conditioner.

Stuck out there in the middle of a field, the school had no protection from the prairie wind, and a chain clanged mournfully against the bare flagpole. It looked and sounded just like a jail. I tried to picture it in the winter and couldn't imagine how it could be any worse. Momma nudged me along to the door.

Inside, there were no signs telling where the office was. Well, of course not, everyone knew. I was probably the first new student in the school in eighty generations. Maybe more. We finally found the office.

"My daughter's here to register," Momma said.

A secretary, fighting a losing battle with the papers blowing around on her desk, snapped, "In the gym."

We went looking for the gym. The Fourteen, of course, were already there when we found it. A coach-like teacher in a white short-sleeved shirt said, "Name?"

"Chandler."

He flipped through some cards.

"Bedelia?"

"No, Dovi."

"No Debbie here."

"I'm not here. I mean, I'm not there. I'm . . . new." I was ashamed to have this overheard, not that the Fourteen couldn't tell already.

"Mrs. Englebrecht," the coach-type yelled across the gym, "we've got a new student here!" Mrs. Englebrecht came gliding over and landed on me eagerly, like a vampire who's just discovered a plump, fresh neck.

"Hello, hello, hello," she chirped. "Where are you from?"

Well, that was a tough question. Did she have an

hour for my whole life story, or did she mean where was I living?

"I was in eighth grade in Wichita," I said.

"Wonderful! We shall have to send for your records."

Momma pulled out a neatly printed list of all my schools, their addresses, and my immunization records from three states. Mrs. Englebrecht was speechless. We couldn't have done more harm if we'd choked her with a gym sock. She handed me a yearbook to glance through while she studied my amazing records.

The girls in the yearbook all had the same hairstyle, and there weren't any black or Asian faces to be seen. The teachers looked like they'd sprouted from the limestone slabs and hadn't ever been kids. I flipped to the Blue and Gold Society picture, where all the top leaders of the school were crammed together on the bleachers in the gym, wearing cute little tams on their heads.

Biscuits and red-eye gravy would have been less nauseating.

"Let's get out of here, Momma," I whispered.

She shot me a stern look as she wrote out the check for enrollment. Well, I signed everything they stuck in front of me, and I picked six classes, though I'm not sure which ones they were.

Despite the enormous steer painted on the floor of

the gym and the horns hanging all over the place, I was utterly sure I did not want to be a Baby Cow after all. In fact, I had no intention of setting foot in Spinner Joint Union High School again. It was so — forever.

Momma and I rode home in silence, and I couldn't wait to tell Stephanie about the school. I was dreaming up ways of making it hilariously funny. A longhorn steer on the floor! Mrs. Englebrecht! Signs on the walls saying ABSOLUTELY NO CHEWING TOBACCO ALLOWED ON PREMISES! I pictured Stephanie rolling around on the floor, clutching her side.

But what I found instead was a pitiful blob of whimpering flesh — Stephanie with her heart broken clean in two. She didn't think she'd survive three days, with this misery. It was worse than Papaya's tragedy, worse even than anything Honorée ever suffered through: Eddie Perini had gotten his orders. He was going to Munich, Germany, to run the Army's radios there.

"It is positively cruel of the Army," Stephanie wailed, "to break up two people in love."

"That's the Uncle for you," Johnny said, not exactly oozing sympathy. "At least he probably won't get shot up, in Germany."

"I — will — never — get over this," Stephanie said. "We're going to write every day."

"It'll cost you a fortune in stamps. You'll have to take

a part-time job when school starts," I teased. "So, is Wayne Firestone starting to look good again?"

"Dovi Chandler, you are crass and rude and insensitive," cried Stephanie.

"That's her specialty," Johnny agreed. "Next to pigs, she likes rudeness best. In fact, I'll bet she's wild about rude pigs, like those two up there on that wall." He pointed to the poster of Sweeney and Petunia rubbing snouts ecstatically and bumping each other's pork chops.

The lovers only set Stephanie off again. "The worst of it is, I won't be able to finish my fiction novel," she wailed. "I'm much too heartsick to create."

Well, that was a big loss to the literary world. I was hoping the gentleman English teacher would come back so I could spread the good news.

With Eddie shipping out any day, there wasn't much to keep Stephanie at the Pig-Out any longer. So she made plans to go home and have her parents take her to Steak and Ale, where she could drown her sorrows in medium rare sirloin.

Momma and I sat in the ripped booth, talking about all this. She absently picked cotton stuffing out of the cushion, and I recognized the look in her eyes. "Stephanie's leaving, and Tag's gone, and school will be starting next month. After the summer, things will slow down around here," she said. "We'll have a quick, cool fall, and how many drivers will be on the road in the dead of winter?"

"Things still have to get from one place to another, like you're always saying." I had to remember to take Momma to meet Mr. Malroy.

"I know, I know, but we'll feel the slowdown. Everything slows down for the winter. Animals and birds and trees. Why not the trucking industry?"

"I'm getting the idea of where you're headed, Momma, but I need more clues. What exactly's on your mind?"

"Don't you think we could use a winter venture, Dov? Somewhere warm. Florida? No, too many retired people there, though the Haitian refugees could use some help. How about Arizona? Or Texas!"

"Doing what?" I asked, already seeing the brown mountains of El Paso spread out before us, the clogged streets of Houston, the hotels along the river in San Antonio. I looked out the window of the Pig-Out, toward the high school I'd never have to set foot in again.

Momma stuffed a wad of cotton back into the cushion. "Oh, I'm just daydreaming. You know me. No one would buy the Pig-Out Inn anyway," Momma said, giving me one of her supremely discontented sighs.

"Well, we could try to find a buyer," I said hopefully.

"Your father would have a heart attack if we did this to him again."

"You saw that school, Momma. He wouldn't want me there."

"Never judge a book by its cover, Dovi," Momma said, but not very convincingly.

"But you saw it from the inside. Would you and Dad want to go to Parents' Night there? Would you want Mrs. Englebrecht cheerfully calling you to bake cupcakes for the Blue and Gold banquet?"

"You're no good for me, Dovi. You cater to my weaknesses," Momma said sadly. "It's time I settled down and grew up." Momma looked around the Pig-Out, at the identical booths with napkin and sugar and hot pepper dispensers, and salt and pepper shakers, and ketchup and mustard bottles arranged in the same neat pattern on each table. "I am not afraid of tornadoes or rats or being poor, but, Dovi, I am terrified of boredom."

SEVENTEEN

wwwwwwwwwwwwwwwwwwwwwwwwwwwwwwwwwwwwwwwwwww

The next day's mail brought a letter from the Omaha
modeling agency, Flair, Inc.

> *Dear Ms. Chandler:*
>
> *I think you may have the very hands we're
> seeking for a jewelry store commercial. Please
> arrange to come to Omaha, at your own expense,
> for a final review of your hands, after which we
> might possibly be in a position to offer you a
> modest contract.*
>
> *We are widely known throughout the Midwest.
> We tell our clients, "For just the right look, send
> up a Flair." Remember, Ms. Chandler, Madison
> Avenue scouts are always monitoring locally
> produced commercials. It is possible that your
> involvement with Flair, Inc. could be parlayed into
> a lucrative national contract.*
>
> *And remember also, you need not have the face
> or the body to go with the hands.*

*I shall look forward to meeting you as soon
as possible.*

Sincerely yours,
Mae Evans Bannister

Once again, before Stephanie jumped ship, we left Johnny in charge and Momma and I drove to Omaha. I slept a lot of the way, with a scarf over my face to keep the dust out of my mouth. When I was awake, I used up about half a bottle of rosewater-and-glycerine on my valuable hands. I daydreamed about seeing these hands of mine on all three major networks. I pictured a fifty-year-old woman with streaks of gray in her hair. She'd wear a lavender organdy apron over her cocktail dress and talk about how new lemon-scented Dish Delight is so good to her hands. The camera would zoom in on her gnarled, arthritic fingers, then show her in Dish Delight up to her elbows, then pan to thirty flipping pages of the calendar — and her never out of the dishwater all those days — and finally, ta-dah! My hands would wave under the nose of the camera, proving to every housewife and bachelor out in TV land that Dish Delight is a miracle! I'd use Dominique as my professional name. Dominique fit hands like mine.

Momma interrupted my lucrative national career. "I wonder if Johnny would buy the Pig-Out."

"Johnny? He hasn't got two quarters to rub together."

"You're right." Miles sped by. The sun played tricks and made us believe there were puddles of water on the road ahead, which was actually so hot that the asphalt turned soft as putty. And then Momma got an inspiration. "What do you think of this, Dovi? Say we leave Johnny in charge for the winter, and we go somewhere else for a few months."

"For the whole school year," I said, "or no deal." I was getting too old to do half a year in one school and half a year somewhere else.

"Oh, of course, for the whole school year."

Why not? I wasn't about to sacrifice my life and be sentenced to four years at Spinner Joint Union High School. I didn't need cows. Why not a school in some other town in Kansas? Why not a school in some other state? Was there anything wrong with Mexico?

We were just south of the Nebraska border, outside of Concordia. Momma's throat was dry, and it was time for lunch anyway. "Let's pull into that truck stop," Momma suggested. "It can't be bad. Look at all the diesels parked there." Walking into the Y Cafe was just like going home for me, but I could tell it made Momma even more restless.

A waitress with blue-black hair way darker than her

eyebrows came up to us with her order book and pencil poised, but she didn't say a word.

Momma whispered, "See, she wears a uniform. Maybe if we'd had uniforms . . ."

The uniform in question fit her better last year, I thought. And I wondered how on earth she folded the hankie sticking out of her breast pocket to look like a nest of butterflies.

"Cheeseburger," I said, "barely breathing, hold the mayo, fries, burn 'em." She wrote it down in that peculiar waitress shorthand we all use, then stared at Momma. Suddenly Momma was in one of her playful moods.

"Do you have beef stroganoff? I didn't see it on the menu."

"Are you kiddin'?"

"No stroganoff. Well, how about chicken cordon bleu?"

"The only bluh thing we got is bluhberry pie, but it ain't today's."

"Is your soup homemade?" Momma asked.

"Sure. Homemade Campbell's. Listen, maybe you should go into town to the Holiday Inn."

"No," Momma said quickly. "I'll just have a chicken salad san, hold the chips, small dinner salad with thousand island, and cup of decaf, black and served with my meal. Both of us on one check, please."

The waitress looked Momma over with some admiration. "Say, you must be a working girl yourself."

While we waited for our lunch and Momma admired my perfect half-moon cuticles for the hundredth time that day, we talked about things we seldom got to. In the next booth there was a family overflowing with children — one in a highchair, one in a booster chair, one on her knees tuning into our conversation — and there were crackers and spoons flying all over the table.

"Children," Momma muttered. "They should be caged until they get to a civilized age. Eleven, I think, is the age of reason." Funny Momma should say such a thing, when she had such a natural way with Tag.

"I've always wonderd, Momma, why didn't you have any other children?"

"Oh, I don't know. We've always led such a nomadic life. Dad and I were just never sure another child would fit in as well as you have."

I had? Well, sure, I always went along with the moves; Momma's enthusiasm rubbed off on me, and I trusted her to stumble across some crazy adventure around every bend. I never wanted things to be ordinary and predictable; just secure.

"Here's the thing, Dovi. What if we'd had a boy and he had some typically male attachment to the land? Can you honestly picture us as alfalfa farmers?"

Farmers!

There were a couple of kids about Stephanie's age huddled on one side of a booth, and despite the Kansas heat, the girl wore the guy's navy blue Windbreaker that said FUTURE FARMERS OF AMERICA in big gold letters on the back. Like Tag's belt buckle. I pictured these two in forty years, rocking on the porch of their farmhouse. Maybe a few geese would be honking around, and the girl-woman would look just the same, only plumper, and the boy-man would look just the same, but with his hide toughened by the wide open sky. How romantic, I thought. Never mind Papaya and Honorée. Stephanie could write a book about these two right here.

But no, I didn't want to be a farmer. I didn't want a plot of stubborn land, and all the worries about rain and bugs and having to chop down the milo — or dig it up, or pick it, or whatever it is farmers do at harvest time — and fighting weeds. It's just that every so often I got this urge to stay put in one place; but I knew that if I came right out and said that, Momma would break out in a cold sweat and welts.

I also wanted to move on, but if I said *that* Momma would have some new scheme cooking for us by nightfall — a trailer park in Alamogordo, maybe.

"No, I can't see us as farmers," I told Momma. "But there's not really anything wrong with having roots." Momma recoiled as if I'd said leprosy, herpes, maggots. "Is it so bad to plant yourself somewhere?" I asked.

"Somewhere, no. But at a truck stop in Podunk, Kansas?"

"Okay, not in Podunk. Where, then? You said it was right for Tag to have a dependable home. What about you and Dad? What about me?"

Momma surveyed the decaying interior of the Y Cafe, so much like our own Pig-Out Inn. "I could learn to live in Spinner," Momma conceded, without much enthusiasm, and though my heart jumped and I dared to imagine for a second what it would be like to start and finish high school in the same building (I'd get used to it, if I had to), I also saw Momma's mind racing way ahead of us both. She was thinking something like this: sure, we'll stay in Spinner. But we'll gut the silly pink booths and the counter, which is chipped anyway, and take down the pigs, and put in shelves, big wide shelves, and a bunch of thick, seasoned wood barrels for pickles or bulghur wheat, and what we'll have is an old-fashioned store. Spinner General Store. Then we'll franchise and move to St. Louis. General Stores all across the prairie.

Our sandwiches came and we got down to the serious business of eating. After a while I said, "Alamogordo?"

"What, Dov?"

"Have you considered Alamogordo?"

"New Mexico? Do you know, that's one state I've never even been in. Lord, and it has mountains and vast deserts and tumbleweeds." She caught her breath and bit the pudgy part of her finger. "Wouldn't you just love to live in an adobe house? Imagine Indian rugs hanging on whitewashed walls. And pottery. We'd only eat off real Indian pottery. Oh, they must have computer places there for Dad, don't you think? Near Santa Fe, maybe? New Mexico is a peace-loving state, I can just feel it. It feels so — so right for us, Dovi."

We were back in the car, the only car along the road for miles and miles. Momma dreamed her way across the great state of New Mexico, and I looked back down the yardstick highway toward the Y Cafe growing smaller and more unreal behind us. Between us and the restaurant there wasn't a building in sight — and ahead, not a grain elevator, not a silo, not a farmhouse, not even a cow or pig as far as the eye could see. Just highway and fields, in shades so green and golden you almost had to shut your eyes when you raced past them. I half expected the Scarecrow With No Brain to pop up in a distant field, but he never did. I glanced at Momma and sensed things clicking away in her head.

Nothing out here but highway and empty wheat fields, I thought, wheat giving way to corn the closer we got to Nebraska, and a blue sky with whipped-cream clouds.

But the sky of New Mexico would be just as blue, and up in the mountains we'd be a whole lot closer to it. And who knew what adventure might be waiting for us around the winding mountain roads of New Mexico, or in the dusty desert? I was ready to give up the Kansas wheat and sunflowers. Weren't we Chandlers more like the tumbleweeds of the desert anyway?